THE LAST CHANCE DETECTIVES

Canyon Quest

Mystery Lights of Navajo Mesa

Legend of the Desert Bigfoot

Escape from Fire Lake

Terror from Outer Space

Revenge of the Phantom Hot Rod

THE
LAST CHANCE
DETECTIVES

Revenge of the Phantom Hot Rod

A Focus on the Family book published by Tyndale House Publishers, Carol Stream, Illinois 60188.

Cover design by Mike Harrigan

For manufacturing information regarding this product, please call 1-855-277-9400.

For information about special discounts for bulk purchases, please contact Tyndale House Publishers at csresponse@tyndale.com, or call 1-855-277-9400.

ISBN 978-1-64607-068-8

Printed in the United States of America

28 27 26 25 24 23 22
7 6 5 4 3 2 1

REVENGE OF THE PHANTOM HOT ROD

ROBERT VERNON

FOCUS ON THE FAMILY®

A Focus on the Family Resource
Published by Tyndale House Publishers

Chapter 1

Ambrosia, Arizona–1995

Arlene Bell let out a deep sigh as she drove her white Ford Fiesta past the neon lights of the Last Chance Diner and onto the stretch of old Route 66 that headed east into the vast, empty desert. It was well past eight o'clock, and she just wanted to get home after a long day at the sheriff's office.

Arlene had served as Sheriff Smitty's radio dispatcher and office manager for almost seven years now, but she had never worked as hard as she had that day. The state auditor was scheduled to visit the next morning, and Arlene was tasked with making sure the filing system containing the past year's arrest reports and traffic citations was in proper order.

She turned her car off 66 and onto the US 191 cutoff, a path that eventually headed north to the long-abandoned ghost town of Jubilee. The old road wound like a snake through the desolate volcanic hills as it gained elevation. Wild burros still wandered through the canyons and sometimes onto the road—the only remaining descendants of the once-thriving mining community.

Arlene had lived in Ambrosia most of her forty-one years, but had recently moved out of the town proper after buying a small mid-century house a few miles beyond the county line. The modest, one-story home had been repossessed by the bank and the price was just too good to pass up.

Her daily drive to work was longer than her previous commute, but Arlene didn't mind. There was usually little to no traffic on the road—except when a movie studio was filming over at the old ghost town, which was rare. Besides, the longer drive gave her a chance to listen to her favorite music. Arlene *loved* movie soundtracks, especially the soundtrack to *Casablanca*, which she was listening to right now. She found the main music theme to be utterly soothing and comforting.

But right now she couldn't afford to get *too* relaxed. After such an exhausting day at the office, she didn't want to fall asleep at the wheel.

Arlene snapped off the music and tried to concentrate on the dark, winding road ahead. It was then that she noticed something in her rearview mirror—the headlights of a fast-approaching car. Arlene lightly pressed on the accelerator and checked the Fiesta's speedometer to make sure she wasn't exceeding the posted speed limit of fifty miles per hour.

The car behind her quickly caught up, its headlights blindingly bright.

"Looks like someone's in a mighty big hurry," she said to herself as she adjusted her mirror to keep the glare out of her eyes.

As the car behind her continued to inch closer, Arlene became aware of a loud, low rumble. Whoever was back there had a lot of horses under that hood. The car was now only a few feet from her rear bumper.

"Oh, c'mon! No tailgating!" she complained out loud. "Could you be any more rude?"

The car behind her revved its engine and surged even closer.

Arlene noticed a straight patch of road ahead, lowered her driver's side window, and waved for the other car to pass. "Just go around! Go around!"

The other car stuck to her bumper, showing no intention of passing.

"What is your problem?" Arlene lisped. Arlene always had a slight lisp, but it became much more noticeable when she was nervous. "Oh, please! I am *waaaay* too tired to be playing games at this time of night."

Arlene only wanted to get home, take her nightly bubble bath, snuggle into her queen-sized bed with her cat, Bogie, and read a chapter or two of her latest romance novel before nodding off to sleep.

Noticing that the road widened up ahead, Arlene came up with a plan to defuse the situation.

"All right, if you won't pass, then I'll just let you by!" she said to the car behind her.

Arlene turned on her right turn signal and pulled off onto the shoulder.

"Have at it! The road's all yours!" she yelled as she slowed to a stop.

She didn't expect the car behind her to pull over and come to a stop as well. But that's exactly what it did.

"What in the world . . ." Arlene said to herself, momentarily stunned.

The other car idled motionless on the shoulder directly behind her, its engine rumbling in the night. A sense of dread began to creep over Arlene. Sheriff Smitty had warned her that some drivers could act irrationally when they were angered. "Road rage" is what he called it.

But I did nothing wrong, she thought. *Certainly nothing to make anyone angry.*

Arlene looked out her rear window to see if anyone got out of the car, but no one did. The car's headlights just stared back at her.

What if it's some kind of serial killer? a voice in her head warned. *And you out here all by yourself!*

She swallowed hard and kept her eyes on the car in her mirror. Still no movement.

It could be coincidental, a more hopeful voice suggested. Maybe the other driver just needed to pull over as well. Or perhaps the other driver noticed something wrong with her car and was trying to get her attention. But if that was the case, then why the silent treatment?

"Oh, fiddlesticks!" Arlene lisped. She couldn't stand the building tension any longer, so she turned on her turn signal, put her car into drive, and eased back onto the highway.

Her heart sank when she saw the other car following right behind her. Soon it was once again moving close to her rear bumper.

"He's playing with me!" Arlene said aloud. She was surprised by how scared her own voice sounded.

What if whoever's back there follows me all the way back to my house? she wondered. *Then he'll know where I live!*

Arlene was familiar enough with the road ahead to know that there were no more turnouts until she reached her home. She was kicking herself for not turning around when she had the chance. She could have pulled a simple U-turn and headed back to the safety of town. To turn around now on the narrow road would require a three-point turn, which would make her vulnerable to whoever was following her. Probably not a smart thing to do on a treacherous two-lane highway in any situation. Arlene decided she had no choice but to continue forward.

She couldn't even tell what kind of car was following her. The headlights were much too bright to make out any details. Besides, the other car was getting so close that Arlene was certain it would nudge her rear bumper at any moment.

If only there were some way to get in touch with Smitty!

Arlene wished she had one of those newfangled cell phones, but not a lot of cell towers had been installed yet, and the coverage was spotty at best in and around the small desert town of Ambrosia. Months ago she had refused Sheriff Smitty's suggestion that she install a police radio scanner in her car. She liked to leave her work at the office.

The car behind her suddenly lurched into the passing lane. The engine revved as it accelerated forward.

"Finally!" Arlene yelled. "Go ahead and pass!"

Arlene stuck out her chin and kept her eyes focused on the road ahead. She wouldn't give the stinky motorist a chance to shoot her any dirty looks as he went by. In fact, she planned to memorize his license plate as soon as he passed and report him to Smitty for reckless driving.

But he didn't pass.

Though she was doing her best to ignore him, Arlene's

peripheral vision told her that the car was now directly alongside and keeping the exact same pace. She could almost feel a pair of eyes staring at her. A chill ran up her spine.

"Just go on. Pass me," she whispered. "Please!"

Another half mile went by. The car beside her was beginning to inch closer and closer. Arlene couldn't stand it any longer. She just had to look over and see who was behind this.

The night was clear and the moon was full, giving Arlene a crystal clear view of the vehicle next to her. The car sported a dark finish with a lot of chrome. Arlene recognized it as some kind of souped-up hot rod that kids used to race in the 1950s, but she couldn't identify the make or model.

When she finally looked at the driver, her mouth dropped open.

There was no one behind the wheel.

Arlene's mind told her that what she saw—that what she *thought* she saw—couldn't possibly be true. It had to be a mistake, perhaps a trick of the summer moonlight. She decided to take a second look.

The car was indeed empty, but the steering wheel was moving on its own, as if guided by some unseen force. Arlene glanced back and forth between the road and the driverless car as she tried to make sense of what she was witnessing.

But what she saw next was just too much. Arlene's face contorted in horror and she let loose a bloodcurdling scream. She hit the brakes hard and was aware of the sound of screeching tires. Her head began to swim, and then—though she tried to fight it—everything went black. Arlene slumped forward in a dead faint. With her foot still on the brakes, her car slowly rolled to a stop.

Chapter 2

HISTORIC ROUTE 66 had once been the main artery across America, running from the sparkling shores of California to the Windy City of Chicago. Along the way, its picturesque path took road-weary travelers through the small, dusty town of Ambrosia. From the mid-1920s to the mid-1950s, the humble settlement was a thriving oasis, offering the only gas, food, and lodging for a hundred miles in either direction.

The construction of Interstate 40 in the 1970s rerouted traffic away from the town, leaving Ambrosia an all but forgotten victim of modern progress. Businesses soon dried up and the town became a shadow of its former self.

Now Ambrosia was more of a curiosity than a necessity for motorists. Tourists who wanted to stay at the Wig-Wam Motor

Lodge or watch a drive-in movie nestled in an ancient meteor crater still stopped by, but not in nearly the same numbers as before.

One business that continued to cater to such clientele was the Last Chance Gas and Diner. A combination gas station and restaurant, the quaint establishment served up the best homestyle entrées in town, and their homemade pies were local favorites. The diner was owned and operated by Roy and Kate Fowler, or "Pop" and "Grandma" as the locals called them.

The Last Chance Gas and Diner was situated near the edge of town, and Pop knew he needed some kind of attraction to lure tourists out that far. So he bought the B-17 Flying Fortress he had piloted in World War II from a governmental surplus scrapyard. He completely refurbished the *Lady Liberty* to its original gleaming aluminum glory and parked it near the diner. Hundreds of tourists stopped by each month to have their picture taken alongside the old warbird. They especially liked to pose near the glass-domed front of the plane, which featured two .50-caliber machine guns poking out of its chin turret. Once they finished marveling at the old plane, they often felt inclined to fill up their gas tanks and get a bite to eat before continuing on their journey.

This particular evening, business was beginning to taper off at the diner and patrons were headed out to their cars. Had they been paying attention, they would have noticed a dim light shining inside the old B-17. Shadows moved back and forth in its warm glow.

That's because Pop Fowler had allowed his thirteen-year-old grandson, Mike Fowler, to use the plane as a makeshift clubhouse.

Mike's father, who was an Air Force fighter pilot, had disappeared during a top-secret mission in the Middle East. Mike was now trying to hone his detective skills in the hope that he might one day discover what had happened to his dad and maybe even finally bring him home.

In the meantime, Mike had formed the Last Chance Detectives with a few of his friends. Together they took on cases ranging from missing pets to uncovering an international smuggling ring. At first many townspeople viewed the Last Chance Detectives as little more than a joke. But after Mike and his friends made national headlines with their exploits, people began taking them seriously.

Tonight they were seated in their customary seats inside the *Lady Liberty*, huddled around an old card table as they concluded their weekly meeting.

◆ ◆ ◆

"So that pretty much wraps up the status report on all our current cases," Mike said as he looked over his notebook. Dressed in his trademark leather flight jacket, Mike was the leader of the group and typically ran their meetings. "Let's do a quick round-robin before we adjourn. Spence, what are you working on?"

"Oh! Can I go first?" Ben Jones asked. He was practically bouncing in his chair.

"You went first last week," Winnie Whitefeather said flatly.

"I know! But wait until you see—"

"She's right, Ben," Mike interrupted. "It's Spence's turn. Go ahead, Spence."

Spence adjusted his glasses and held up a small metal container. "I've been working on this superstrong adhesive compound."

Young Spencer Martin was a walking encyclopedia and was always coming up with imaginative inventions. Yet this time no one seemed to be very impressed.

Ben examined the metal container and sniffed the contents. "Pew!" he said. "It's basically superglue. Someone already invented that."

"This is better," Spence said confidently.

"In what way?" Mike asked.

"It bonds almost immediately to any surface with a super-strong adhesion that's nearly impossible to break."

Everyone still looked unimpressed.

Winnie picked up the container. "I still don't get it. *Glue?*"

"They want to know the application, Spence," Mike said. "What can we use it for?"

Spence sighed and placed some six-inch wood blocks on the table. Some of the blocks had handles fastened to them. "Okay, let's say you fall into a deep well with no means of climbing out. With my glue, you could instantaneously stick these blocks to the walls and use them to help you climb out."

"Yeah, but who's gonna be carrying around a bunch of blocks in their pocket?" Ben asked. "What if you fell in a well and there was nothing to glue to the walls?"

"If nothing else, you could take off your shirt, pour some of my glue on it, slap it high on the wall, and pull yourself out that way. It sticks to practically anything!"

"And it would hold your weight?" Winnie asked.

"Up to two hundred pounds for at least ten hours," Spence explained. "I'm still working on making it last longer."

"Huh, that might actually come in handy," Mike admitted.

Ben turned to Mike. "Can I go next?"

"It's still not your turn. Go ahead, Winnie."

"I've been working on a memory board." Winnie stood up and presented a two-foot by four-foot bulletin board that had been leaning against the wall. She turned it around to reveal a collection of newspaper clippings of their adventures together. "I thought it might also be a fun place to post things, like cute art we've created."

"Cute art? Oh, brother!" Ben groaned.

Ignoring him, Winnie pulled out a sketch she had drawn of her Navajo grandmother and pinned it to the bulletin board. "Like this."

"Hey, that's really good, Winnie!" Mike exclaimed. "It looks exactly like her."

Slightly embarrassed, Winnie ran her fingers through her long black hair. "Thanks, Mike."

Wynona "Winnie" Whitefeather really was a talented artist. In the past, she had drawn highly detailed composite sketches based on witnesses' descriptions. And each time they were uncannily accurate.

"Wow," Mike said as he examined the picture closer. "You just keep getting better and better!"

Winnie sat back down. "I'm trying to draw a lot more right now so I can improve some of my techniques," she said. "I'm planning to enter a few sketches in the county fair's fine art competition."

"I bet you'll win a ribbon," Spence said.

Ben got up from his chair and pinned his own artwork to the board. Below the word "Winnie" was a crude drawing of a stick figure. "Now that's what I call art!"

"I'm sorry." Winnie looked at him dryly. "Is that supposed to be me?"

"Ha!" Ben usually thought his own jokes were funny even when others did not. "I think it's pretty accurate."

Winnie shook her head and pulled out a chair for Ben. "Just sit down. You're up next."

"About time!" Ben plopped down in his chair. "You guys are gonna love this!"

Cheerful and animated, Ben Jones was always enthusiastic about his own ideas—especially when they involved eating junk food or playing video games. He pointed to his latest issue of *Action Rangers*. "I found a very interesting advertisement in this graphic novel."

"Comic book," Winnie corrected.

"Graphic novel!" Ben shot back. "Anyway, I sent away for a device that gives you the ability to throw your voice."

Ben held up a small V-shaped metal piece with a rubber band around it. "Imagine that we're captured by bad guys, and we need a distraction in order to make our escape. That's where this little baby comes into play."

Ben paused before he slipped the device into his mouth. "Are you guys ready for this? It's awesome!"

"Don't choke on that thing," Mike warned.

Ben signaled for everyone to remain quiet. Mike and the others all leaned forward expectantly.

Trying hard not to move his lips, Ben began to speak out of the side of his mouth: "Thtop in the name uf the law! Thith ith the poleeth! You're all under arrethdt! Thurrender now!"

Ben took the device out of his mouth. "Pretty amazing, isn't it? But don't expect to master it at first. It takes a lot of disciplined training until you're as good as I am. Didn't it sound like my voice came from outside?"

Everyone looked at each other blankly before Mike slowly shook his head. "Not exactly."

Ben was surprised. "Really? Then where did it sound like it came from?"

Mike hated to burst Ben's bubble, so he tried to break the news gently. "It sounded like it came from . . . well . . . from where you're sitting."

"And it sounded like you had a piece of metal and a rubber band in your mouth," Spence added.

Winnie was a bit more blunt: "It was awful."

Ben pondered their reaction, but only for a moment. His eyes lit up as something occurred to him. "I know what the problem is," he said. "I'm sitting too close to you guys. Let me just get a little distance and . . ."

Ben started to stand, but the chair came with him. He was a little thick through the middle (or "husky," as he liked to put it), but certainly not thick enough to get caught between the chair's arms.

"Hold on just a second . . ." Ben tried to push the chair away, but it wasn't going anywhere.

"What's the matter?" Mike asked.

Ben continued to grapple with the chair. "This chair, it won't . . . Wait a minute!"

Ben pulled his hand away from the chair, and they could all see traces of a gooey substance on his fingers. He held it up to his nose and grimaced. "Yuck! I think it's Spence's glue!"

"How did that get there?" Spence asked.

"I'll tell you how it got on there!" Ben angrily wrestled with the chair. "Somebody *put* it there!"

Mike held up his hands. "I didn't do it!"

"Me, neither!" said Spence.

Ben's eyes fell on Winnie, who was doing a poor job of looking innocent.

"Winnie!"

"I was always told that you should look before you sit," Winnie said, trying her best not to laugh.

"*Winnie!*" Ben roared. "When I get out of this . . ." Ben suddenly turned to Spence. "How long did you say this stuff lasts?"

"A good ten hours I'm afraid."

"Great, the glue has seeped all the way through my pants to my skin! This isn't funny! How am I supposed to sleep tonight with this chair stuck back there? Huh?"

Mike shrugged and looked to Spence.

"I guess you'll have to sleep sitting up," Spence said.

Ben shook his rear and the chair waggled around behind him.

Winnie tried not to giggle.

Mike didn't want to laugh, but seeing Ben stand there awkwardly with a chair stuck to his backside *was* pretty hysterical.

"Do you guys find this funny?" Ben fumed.

Winnie couldn't hold it in any longer and burst out laughing. And because laughter is contagious, Mike soon joined her.

"Go ahead and laugh now, Winnie, but I'm gonna get even!"

Winnie wiped away her tears of laughter. "You were the one who started it with that goofy picture!"

"*I* started it? You crank-called my house last week and tricked me into thinking I won a million dollars!"

Mike laughed harder. "She *what*?"

Winnie held her nose to make her voice sound nasal. "Hello, Mr. Jones. You're our grand-prize winner!"

"Just you wait, Winnie! You're gonna get—"

"Hey!" Spence yelled. He looked deadly serious. "Everyone be quiet for a minute. Do you guys hear something?"

It was out of character for Spence to be so forceful, so everyone quickly calmed down and listened.

The sound was faint at first. But after a few moments they could clearly make out the eerie sound of a woman crying. Not just crying; more like wailing. And the sound was coming from just outside the B-17.

Chapter 3

The Last Chance Detectives found Arlene Bell slumped against her car in the diner's parking lot. She was shaking uncontrollably, blubbering incoherently, and mascara ran down her cheeks. Someone or something had obviously put her into a state of shock.

Mike and Winnie helped Arlene to her feet and into the Last Chance Diner. Once Arlene was safely inside, Grandma Fowler took over and made sure the sheriff's dispatcher was as comfortable as possible in a dining booth.

"Can I get you some water? Or something to eat?" Grandma asked.

"No, thank you." Arlene shook her head and wiped her face with a napkin. "I just need to talk to Sheriff Smitty."

"He's on his way!" Pop Fowler called from the pay phone on the back wall.

Grandma pushed her way past the kids who were hovering around the booth. "Everybody, step back and give Arlene some room to breathe. Ben, whatever is that chair doing stuck to your, um, backside?"

"Oh, this thing?" Ben chuckled and tried to act like nothing was out of the ordinary. "It's just one of Spence's science experiments. Crazy kid!"

Mike's mother, Gail, worked at the diner with the rest of the family. She carried a cup and saucer to the table and carefully set it before Arlene.

"At least have a nice warm cup of chamomile tea," Gail encouraged. "I put some honey in it. It'll help you relax."

"Well, I suppose that might help." Arlene tried to raise the cup to her mouth but was still trembling so much that she quickly set it back down.

"That's okay," Gail assured her. "Why don't you tell us what happened?"

"I'd rather wait until Smitty gets here," Arlene said.

"He's just pulling in now," Pop said as a pair of headlights appeared in the diner's front window.

Theodore Smitty had been the sheriff of Ambrosia for some twenty years. He was tall and lanky, wore pressed blue jeans and a tan uniform shirt with a star pinned to his chest. Beneath Smitty's trademark Stetson hat were a pair of slate-gray eyes, a tanned face, and a bushy Wyatt Earp–style mustache. He was visibly concerned when he entered the diner and immediately sat down next to Arlene.

"First, are you okay?" Smitty put his hand on Arlene's, and

she started to cry again. "Just tell me what happened, and then I'll drive you home."

"No!" Arlene was firm. "I'm not going back out there!"

"Okay, no problem. We'll find a place for you to spend the night in town."

"Ben, do you think your folks have room for Arlene at the Wig-Wam Motor Lodge?" Gail asked.

"Sure. Well, I think so," Ben answered.

Smitty turned back to Arlene. "Now, talk to me. What happened out there?"

"It was just awful!"

"I'm sure it was. Start from the beginning."

Arlene struggled to find the words at first as she fought back more tears. Eventually, she recounted the horrible events of that evening—how she had been stalked and terrorized by a mysterious car.

"Did you get a good look at the vehicle?" Smitty took out a pocket notepad and pen. "Can you give me a description?"

"When it pulled up alongside me, I got a pretty good look. The car was dark. Black, I think, or it could've been dark maroon, maybe even a deep blue. I couldn't quite tell. But it was definitely dark in color."

"Uh-huh . . ." Smitty scribbled on his pad.

"It was an older car, but it sounded real powerful. Like one of those souped-up cars teenagers used to race in films like *American Graffiti* or *Rebel Without a Cause*."

"So, it was a dark, vintage hot rod," Smitty clarified.

Arlene nodded. "But I didn't get the license plate, and I don't know the make and model."

"That's okay. What did the driver look like?"

Arlene paused and looked down at the table.

Smitty gave her a moment, then finally asked: "Was it someone you know?"

Arlene silently shook her head.

"Then just do your best to describe him."

Arlene's chin began to tremble, and her eyes welled up with tears again. "You won't believe me."

"I'll do my best," Smitty assured her. "Please. Just tell me what you saw."

"That's just it. I saw nothing at first."

"What do you mean?"

"I know it sounds crazy, but . . . the car was empty. There was no one there."

"No driver?"

Arlene nodded. "The steering wheel just turned back and forth on its own."

At a nearby table, the four kids sat, transfixed on every word.

"You said that you saw nothing *at first*." Smitty leaned in closer. "What did you see after that?"

"Well, this is where it starts to get weird," Arlene admitted.

"*Starts* to get weird?" Ben whispered to Mike.

Arlene continued. "Suddenly the driver was just there!"

Smitty looked up from his notepad. "You mean he sat up from where he was hiding?"

"No. It was as if he just materialized right before my eyes. I mean, I could see right through him!"

Smitty put down the notepad. "Now, hold on a second—"

"You said you would try to believe me," Arlene reminded him.

"I *am* trying to. It's just that it sounds like you're describing a, um . . ." Smitty cleared his throat, ". . . well, a ghost."

"I know." Arlene miserably shook her head. "I know it sounds crazy, but that's what really happened! And that's not the worst of it."

"Go on," Smitty said.

"I hit the brakes and must've passed out because next thing I know, my car's stopped on the side of the road, and . . ." Arlene started sobbing again.

Smitty put his arm around her. "I'm sorry, Arlene, but you've got to tell me so I can help."

"Oh, Smitty! When I was passed out, he, he . . ." Arlene hid her face in her hands. "He got into the car with me!"

Smitty studied her intently. "Why would you think that, Arlene?"

"Because I found something he left behind."

"What? What did he leave?"

Arlene pulled a wadded-up piece of paper from her pocket and handed it to Smitty. "Something for you."

Smitty took the paper and slowly un-wadded it. Three words were written in what everyone hoped was red ink:

SMITTY – YOU'RE NEXT!

◆ ◆ ◆

It was getting close to midnight when everyone finally left the diner.

"So, what did you guys think of all that?" Mike asked the gang.

"It's obvious that Arlene believes everything she's saying," Spence pointed out.

Ben pulled at the chair still stuck to his backside. It wasn't going anywhere. "No disrespect intended, but I'm hoping she's crazy."

"Ben!" Winnie punched him in the arm. "Why would you say something like that?"

"Because I don't want to live in an area where ghosts haunt the highways!"

"And what about that note to Smitty?" Spence asked.

Winnie felt a shiver go down her spine. "It's creepy is what it is."

"One thing's for sure," Mike said. "We just found our next case!"

Chapter 4

The next night found Smitty sitting in his patrol pickup truck, parked behind a dimly lit billboard on US 191. He had both windows down and a radar gun cradled in his arms. Several hours had already passed, yet he'd seen no sign of any ghost-driven hot rod. In fact, only a handful of cars had passed by all night. With the exception of some crickets, he was all alone.

He knew highway 191 well. Back in his teen years, this road was the ideal test track to find out what your car was capable of. There was little to no traffic, and the road featured just the right mix of straightaways, challenging turns, and tiny hills that gave fast drivers the feeling of weightlessness—what his friends liked to call "whoop-de-doos." He had made a lot of good memories here. Some bad ones, too.

Smitty yawned and checked his watch. It was nearing midnight. He decided to give it another ten or fifteen minutes before packing it in for the night.

A moth flew in through the open window and fluttered around inside the cab. Smitty tried to wave it out a few times before he finally made a striking grab. Unsure whether he had actually caught the flying pest, Smitty slowly started to open his fingers. Just as the moth darted from his hand, the police radio squelched to life. The sudden sound startled Smitty, who nearly jumped out of his seat.

"Smitty! Come in, Smitty!"

Smitty let out an exasperated sigh and picked up the mic to respond. "Go ahead, Arlene."

"Is everything okay out there?" She sounded worried.

"Everything's just fine. Same as it was five minutes ago when you checked in. And five minutes before that."

"I'm sorry, but I'm worried about you with that ghost car prowling around—"

"Now, Arlene!" Smitty snapped. "We both know that there's no such thing as ghosts. I wish you'd quit using that word. And I *don't* want you spreading rumors around town that there is such a thing around here."

"Me?"

"Yes, *you*! Everyone knows you have a bad habit of spreading information that may or may not be true."

Arlene didn't answer.

Smitty realized that he had probably hurt her feelings. "Arlene, are you there?"

"Yes." Her voice sounded small and on the verge of tears.

"I'm sorry, Arlene. Listen, I really appreciate you sticking around the office tonight and checking in on me."

"I'm just concerned for your safety is all."

"And I appreciate that. I really do. I . . ."

Smitty leaned over and turned down the volume on the police radio. He could swear that he'd heard something off in the distance. Music, perhaps?

Arlene continued: *"I know you think you can take care of yourself, but I still wish you weren't all alone out there—"*

"Hold on, Arlene," Smitty interrupted. "I'm hearing something."

Smitty opened the door and stepped out of the truck so he could hear better.

"What is it?" Arlene asked.

Smitty could definitely hear music, and it was slowly getting louder. He walked to the center of the road as he tried to get a bearing on the sound's location.

The night crickets stopped chirping. In addition to the approaching music, Smitty became aware of a slow-growing rumble. He knew the sound well—the unmistakable growl of a big-block V8 engine.

The music was louder now. A lazy steel guitar played a familiar but haunting tune.

"I know that song," Smitty whispered to himself. It was "Sleep Walk" by Santo & Johnny, released in 1959.

About sixty yards up the road, a pair of headlights crested the hill and came to a stop. The car literally trembled with horsepower as a blue cloud of exhaust dramatically rose from the tailpipe. It was immediately obvious that the dark vehicle was the source of the music. Smitty knew instinctively that this 1950 Buick Roadmaster was Arlene's phantom car. Its stance was close to the ground, and its chrome bumper looked like gleaming teeth lit from behind with a deep red glow.

Smitty had seen this exact same model just once before, but that was a long, long time ago.

The Buick shook with each rev of the engine. Flames shot out of three portals on each side of the hood. It reminded Smitty of a dragon ready to pounce on its prey.

Realizing he was vulnerable standing in the middle of the road, Smitty started walking back to his truck.

The Roadmaster roared to life, tires spinning as plumes of black smoke rose into the night air. With a squeal of burning rubber, the sedan lurched forward.

Smitty's leisurely walk became a sprint. By the time he climbed inside his truck, the Buick was already roaring past. In one quick move, Smitty started the engine and hit the switch that activated the emergency lightbar on top of the truck.

He immediately radioed Arlene. "Be advised—I'm in pursuit of a black 1950 Buick, heading north on 191."

"Be careful, Smitty!" Arlene radioed back.

There was no way Smitty should've been able to catch the more powerful car, but the Buick had slowed down—as if it was waiting for him. Smitty pulled up behind the Buick and checked his speedometer. Both vehicles were doing well over seventy miles per hour. The flashing police lights lit up the back of the Roadmaster like a Christmas tree.

Smitty turned on his outside speakers and spoke into the mic. "Pull over to the side of the road!"

The Buick replied with a burst of blue flames as the hot rod accelerated.

Smitty picked up his own speed to keep pace. "This is the county sheriff! Pull over!"

The Buick slowed once again, so Smitty veered into the passing lane and pulled up alongside. Though Arlene had told him what to expect, he didn't actually believe it until he saw it with his own eyes.

The car was empty. The steering wheel seemed to turn by itself. From his raised position in the truck, Smitty could see that no one was hiding or crouching in front of the bench seat.

But he did see *something*.

Blue tendrils of smoke started to swirl inside the roadster. They merged together and slowly settled into the form of a ghostly figure. Smitty could make out traces of clothing and even the features of a face.

It was a face he recognized.

"*Jimmy?*" Smitty gasped. "Jimmy Sutton?"

The interior of the Buick suddenly erupted into a blazing inferno. Red hot flames seemed to consume every square inch inside the sedan.

"Oh, no . . ." Smitty groaned. He knew that even the most powerful engines could be pushed too far. Especially when horsepower-boosting nitrous oxide is involved, there is always the risk of too much heat. Convinced he was now witnessing just such a situation, Smitty quickly checked the road ahead.

They were approaching the highway's notorious "Suicide Curve." Whoever or whatever was steering the car could never navigate that turn while engulfed in flames.

Smitty took one last glance inside the Buick alongside

him. The raging flames suddenly vanished as fast as they had appeared. In the driver's seat, a blackened figure clutched the steering wheel with now skeletal fingers. White, marble-like eyes stared back at Smitty, and gristled lips pulled back into a ghastly grin.

Smitty couldn't look away from the figure. For a few seconds he forgot where he was—and that was all it took. By the time he looked ahead, Smitty realized that he was coming up on the sharp curve much faster than he should. He might be able to make the turn if—

The other car veered sharply into Smitty's lane, hitting the pickup hard. The crash was deafening. The sheriff's truck careened away from the Buick with no place to go. Smitty desperately stomped the brake pedal, but it was too late. His truck crashed through the old wooden guardrail and over the shoulder. Smitty defensively threw up his arms as his truck headed for the dark canyon below.

Chapter 5

Thanks to Arlene, by noon the next day word had spread like wildfire across town. Just about everyone in Ambrosia had heard how Smitty was forced off "Suicide Curve" by some kind of phantom hot rod. Whether an actual ghost was driving was hotly debated, but one thing nearly everyone agreed on was that it was a miracle Smitty had somehow survived.

Since the Last Chance Gas and Diner was the closest service station to the scene of the accident, Pop Fowler was assigned the duty of towing out the wreckage. Paramedics had already taken Smitty to the county hospital when Pop and Mike rolled up on the scene.

They could still see Smitty's skid marks and the spot where his truck had crashed through the wooden guardrail.

Fortunately for Smitty, someone in the past had thought to reinforce the old guardrail with a metal safety cable that ran the entire length of the dangerous turn. Although it didn't stop Smitty from careening off the road, the cable did get tangled around his truck's axle—preventing him from plunging to an almost certain death.

Once they had retrieved the patrol truck, Mike and Pop headed to the hospital to check in on Smitty. They found him lying awake in his bed, his head bandaged and his right arm in a sling.

Smitty grimaced as a nurse inserted a needle into his left hip.

"What was that for?" he grumbled.

"It's just an antibiotic." Nurse Burns quickly applied a bandage. "We don't want those cuts and scrapes getting infected, now do we?"

"How are you doing, Smitty?" Pop asked.

"Why do I always end up in here, Pop?" Smitty complained. "I hate hospitals!"

"You should just be grateful that you're still alive," Pop said.

"Are you in a lot of pain?" Mike asked.

"Aw, I broke my ankle, have a sore shoulder, and a slight concussion."

"There's no such thing as a *slight* concussion," the nurse reminded him. "You took a strong blow to the head. That's why we need to keep you here for observation."

"Yeah, but for *two or three* days?"

"That's what Dr. Benson ordered."

Smitty clearly didn't want to discuss it anymore, so he changed the subject. "How's my truck, Pop?"

"Well, I haven't had a chance to look over everything, but I can already tell that it needs a new bumper, plus the panels on the right side need to be banged out. You should probably have the rear wheel bearings checked, too. But it could have been a lot worse."

"Well, that's good." Smitty looked relieved. "But until it gets fixed, I'm gonna need another vehicle. Pop, can you get somebody to drop off my personal car over here?"

"Sure," Pop replied.

"It's the Crown Vic parked behind the sheriff's office. Arlene can get you the keys."

"Smitty . . ." Pop pulled up a chair next to the bed. "Arlene's telling everyone who will listen that you were attacked by the same phantom car that she claims she saw."

Smitty shook his head. "I sure wish she wouldn't spread rumors around town like that! You know how she is. Always telling stories."

"Then what *did* happen, Sheriff?" Mike asked.

"Well, it's . . ." Smitty paused and looked down to avoid eye contact. "I tried to pull somebody over for speeding, he hit the gas, and I got careless. It's that simple."

"The way your truck's right side panels are banged in, it appears that you collided with something," Pop said. "It looks like black paint from another car."

Smitty remained silent and just shook his head.

"So, no one ran you off the road?" Mike asked.

"Look, it was pretty late. I was tired and just misjudged the turn."

"That's all?" Pop asked.

"That's all. It's just too bad the suspect got away before I could identify him."

"Maybe I can help," Nurse Burns volunteered.

"In what way?" Smitty asked.

"Well, last night—when they wheeled you in here—you were drifting in and out of consciousness. You kept mumbling something about a guy. I wrote it down here somewhere . . ."

The nurse flipped through a couple of pages on her clipboard. "Here it is . . . Jimmy Sutton! Yeah, you seemed to be saying something about this Jimmy Sutton character running you off the road. Does that name ring a bell?"

Smitty's forehead furrowed as if deep in thought, but he made no reply.

"Smitty?" Pop asked, looking for some kind of confirmation.

"Guess I must've been hit in the head harder than I thought. Right, Pop?" Smitty forced a laugh. "I mean, you and I both know that it couldn't have been Jimmy Sutton! Right?"

Pop nodded slowly, but the look on his face was very concerned.

◆ ◆ ◆

"That was kind of weird," Mike said to Pop as they left Smitty's room to go pick up the sheriff's car.

"How do you mean?" Pop asked.

"Smitty," Mike said. "It seemed like he was hiding something."

"I got that feeling too."

"I don't think he would lie to us, Pop."

"I don't think so, either. I've known Smitty long enough to

know that lying goes against his code," Pop said. "But I'm not sure he was telling us the whole story."

"Mr. Fowler!" Nurse Burns waved them over to the nurses' station. "There's one other thing."

"Sure. What is it?"

"One of the paramedics who brought Sheriff Smitty in last night—I think his name was Andy—he mentioned seeing an old car drive by as they were loading Smitty into the ambulance. He said that criminals will sometimes revisit the scene of their crime, so he made a mental note of the make and model. Andy must have been sort of a car buff because he knew it was a 1950 Buick Road-something . . ."

"Roadmaster?" Pop asked.

"Yeah, that's it. Said it was black with a lot of chrome."

Pop looked deep in thought. "That's quite a coincidence . . ."

"What is?" Mike asked.

"The last time I saw Jimmy Sutton, he was driving a black 1950 Buick Roadmaster." Pop turned to the nurse. "Please pass that information on to Smitty. He'll want to know."

"I already did," Nurse Burns said. "But he didn't seem interested."

As the nurse returned to her duties, Mike and Pop continued down the hospital corridor.

"I wonder why Smitty ruled out this Jimmy Sutton guy so quickly?" Mike asked Pop. "Maybe someone should ask him where he was and what he was doing last night."

"I'm afraid that would be impossible," Pop said flatly.

"Why? Doesn't anybody know where he is?"

Pop took a deep breath and exhaled slowly. "Oh, I know *exactly* where he is."

◆ ◆ ◆

Twenty minutes later, Mike found himself at Ambrosia's Sunset Vista Cemetery. Pop pointed to a polished gravestone at their feet. The inscription read:

James Sutton
Beloved Son
1946–1965

"Get the picture, Mike?"

Mike nodded. "Who was he?"

"Jimmy was a bit of a legend back in the day. He used to drive a black 1950 Roadmaster. It was the fastest car around these parts. As far as I knew, no one ever beat him in a race—until the day Jimmy tempted fate one too many times. Skidded off the same curve that almost claimed Smitty last night."

Mike stared down at the gravestone. "So Smitty identifies Sutton by name, and the paramedic sees the same car that Jimmy used to drive. Pop, do you believe in—?"

"Ghosts?" Pop shook his head. "Absolutely not."

"But how do you know?"

"The Bible tells us there *is* a spiritual realm that's invisible to human eyes, and that spiritual beings *can* connect with our physical world. But the Bible identifies them only as angels or demons."

"Never ghosts?" Mike asked.

"Nope," Pop said. "Hebrews 9:27 says that men die only once, and after that comes judgment. So, Mike, it's pretty clear that there's no such thing as a ghost."

"Then how do you explain everything that's happened?"

Pop shrugged. "It's a mystery to me, Mike."

As they turned to head back to the truck, Pop put an arm around his grandson's shoulder.

"You wouldn't happen to know anyone who does detective work, would you?"

Chapter 6

As soon as Mike returned to the diner, he got on the phone and called an emergency meeting of the Last Chance Detectives. Within an hour, Winnie, Ben, and Spence had joined him in the B-17.

Mike quickly filled them in on everything he had learned that morning. He even drew a map of highway 191, with special detail paid to the infamous "Suicide Curve."

Winnie paced back and forth as she listened. "So you don't think Smitty was being truthful about what happened?"

"I wouldn't say he was lying," Mike explained. "Pop and I just don't know if he was telling us the whole story."

"You mean maybe he was hiding something?" Spence asked.

"That's *exactly* what I mean." Mike pointed to the map.

"And that's why I think it's so important to visit the site of Smitty's accident to see if we can find any more clues before they disappear."

Winnie leaned over the table to examine the map. "Where exactly is that turn again?"

Ben politely pulled out a chair for her to sit in. "Please, have a seat."

Winnie stood her ground and glared at him. "Nice try. You don't think I'm that stupid, do you?"

"What do you mean?" Ben batted his eyes innocently.

"I bet you put some of Spence's glue on my seat, didn't you?"

"Of course not!" Ben looked hurt by the accusation.

"I know what you're up to. You just want to get even."

"C'mon, guys!" Mike said. "We've got an urgent case here that we need to solve. This is no time for practical jokes."

"Don't look at me," Ben said. "I was just trying to be a gentleman."

"Let's just see about that." Winnie crouched down to examine the seat. It was clean.

"See!" Ben said with a look of vindication.

Winnie eyed him suspiciously as she sat down. "I still say you're up to something."

"Okay, back to business," Mike said. "With Smitty laid up in the hospital, it's up to us to get to the bottom of this mystery."

"What happened to his deputy?" Spence asked.

"He's on vacation," Mike explained. "Which means Smitty has to rely on his second reservist, Howard Falfa. Everybody knows that guy does the least amount of work possible."

"So it really *is* up to us." Winnie looked worried. "To be honest, I'm afraid for Smitty. Once this phantom driver learns that he failed the first time, who's to say he won't come after Smitty again?"

"That's why time is of the essence." Mike picked up a clipboard. "I've written down some assignments for each of us. I think we should split up, find out as much as we possibly can, and meet back here tomorrow morning."

Spence nodded. "That's a good plan."

"Spence, I'd like you to do some research on this Jimmy Sutton character. Where was he born? What was his family like? Who were his friends? Did he ever get in trouble with the law? That kind of thing."

"No problem," Spence said.

Mike examined his clipboard again. "Winnie, I'd like you to find this paramedic who thinks he may have spotted the phantom car. The nurse thought his name was Andy. Locate him if you can and see if you can get any more information."

"On it," Winnie replied.

"Ben and I are gonna ride our bikes out to Suicide Curve and scour the place for any further clues. Maybe there are some tire tracks in the dirt we can identify. Ben, you should borrow your mom's Polaroid camera just in case."

"Okay," Ben agreed.

"And one more thing . . ." Mike looked at his friends intently. "We need to work together as a team. Catch my drift, Ben and Winnie? No more feuds."

"I couldn't agree more," Winnie said. "I call for a truce, Ben." She elbowed Ben in the ribs and giggled. "Especially now that I'm ahead."

Everyone expected Ben to go ballistic, but he calmly smiled and pulled out a gift-wrapped cylinder. "I agree, Winnie. It's time we quit this silly contest of practical jokes once and for all. And as a token of my goodwill, I'd like for you to have this as a peace offering."

Winnie picked up the cylinder and looked at it sourly. "Do you really think I'm that big of a ninny? That I can't tell what this is?"

Ben's smile faded.

Winnie tore back a corner of the gift wrapping to reveal the words: "Can O' Snakes." She rolled her eyes.

"I suppose you think I just fell off the turnip truck and have never seen a magician's can of spring-loaded 'snakes' before."

Ben's face began to flush in embarrassment.

"Are you telling me that this is the best you could come up with?" she asked.

Ben hung his head in shame.

Winnie could only shake her head. "You continue to disappoint even my low expectations."

She didn't notice when Ben pulled on a hidden monofilament line. A plug came out of the bottom of the tube, and a clown beetle dropped out and onto Winnie's lap.

Mike and Spence saw what had happened, but Winnie was oblivious.

"I mean, fake spring-loaded snakes are one of the oldest tricks in the book!" she continued.

The beetle started crawling up the front of Winnie's overalls.

"Um, Winnie . . ." Mike tried to interrupt. "There's a—"

"Hold on, Mike." Winnie wasn't done with Ben just yet. "At least show a little originality. Maybe just a little creativity. A little . . ."

The words caught in Winnie's throat as she noticed Ben

trying not to laugh as he pointed at her front. That's when she felt the horrifying tickle of insect legs on her neck. She instinctually brushed the bug away, and it tumbled onto her lap. The clown beetle deftly flipped over, reared up on its hind legs, and let loose with a loud, stinky hiss.

In the confines of the B-17, Winnie's ear-splitting scream was absolutely deafening. Mike wouldn't have been surprised if the lenses in Spence's glasses had actually shattered.

In her panicked effort to get as far away from the beetle as possible, Winnie overturned the card table, upended chairs, and sent their new bulletin board crashing to the floor. As the screaming continued, Mike and Spence miserably clapped their hands to their ears and did their best to dodge the flying furniture.

But none of it bothered Ben. He sat back in his chair and basked in the warm, satisfying glow of *payback*.

Chapter 7

It took Mike and Ben nearly an hour to pedal out to highway 191. When they finally arrived, they had both worked up quite a sweat. They parked their bikes on the side of the road, and Mike took a long drink from his canteen.

"Don't we still have a ways to go until Suicide Curve?" Ben asked.

"It's a couple hundred yards ahead, but I thought we should start walking from here and each take one side of the road." Mike crossed to the opposite side of the highway. "Scan the pavement and dirt shoulder of the road for any clues."

"Just what are we looking for?" Ben asked as he stared at the ground.

"I don't know exactly. But we'll know it when we see it." Mike walked slowly, his eyes carefully scanning the pavement and the dirt shoulder. "Have you ever heard of the Police Explorers?"

"Nope," Ben replied. "What is it?"

"Police departments all over the country have this program for kids who are interested in law enforcement. You have to have finished the sixth grade to join, but you get to help solve real crime cases."

"That sounds kinda cool," Ben admitted.

"Well, one of their jobs is doing exactly what we're doing now."

"They look for stuff on the side of the road?" Ben kicked a tin can out of his way.

"Yep. Sometimes suspects will toss evidence or weapons out of their car before they're arrested. It's up to the Explorers to find it."

"They must get hungry," Ben said. He took off his overstuffed backpack and studied its contents. "You want any of this?"

"What have you got in there?"

"Chips, pretzels, popcorn, candy, gum."

"What kind of candy?"

"Just about every candy bar you could think of." Ben rummaged through the backpack and took stock of its contents. "Plus Gummi Giraffes, Pixie Puckers, Red Hotties, Jawbreakers, Fizz Wizz, Super Sour Slimes, Nuclear Cinnamon Bombs, Pop Pebbles, Wacky Taffy, Kandy Ka-Booms—"

"Wait a minute!" Mike interrupted. "Why in the world would you buy all that junk?"

"Because of that crazy Winnie!" Ben exclaimed. "Remember, she tricked me into thinking I had won a million dollars. So I naturally spent all my savings on candy."

"That was unfortunate."

"Yeah," Ben said. "Turns out you can't return this stuff."

Both boys continued to scan the roadside for clues.

"You know, you two really need to stop your feuding," Mike said.

"Winnie just gets on my nerves sometimes. Besides, she started it."

"I thought you kinda liked Winnie."

"Me?" Ben acted shocked.

"Yeah, didn't you admit once that you had a crush on her?"

"On *Winnie*?" Ben feigned a vague recollection. "I might have said that back when I was a goofy little kid."

"Ben, that was a few months ago," Mike reminded him. "So, do you still like her?"

Ben ignored the question and stared at the ground. "What's this?"

"Nice try," Mike said. "Answer the question."

"No, I mean it." Ben crouched down for a closer look. "This broken glass on the ground looks fresh."

Mike walked across the road and joined Ben. "You're right! And there's where Smitty's skid marks begin before he went through the guardrail."

"But if there's glass back here . . ."

Mike finished his sentence for him. "Then somebody must have hit Smitty as they tried to drive him off the road!"

Ben's foot stepped on a rusted rectangular piece of metal partially covered with dirt. "Check this out, Mike. You know what I bet this is?"

Ben picked up the object, and Mike's eyes widened.

"A license plate!" they both exclaimed in unison.

◆ ◆ ◆

A slim, twenty-eight-year-old man dressed in a paramedic's uniform sat at the Last Chance Diner's counter, digging into a steaming bowl of chili. Winnie approached him and extended her hand. "Hi, are you Andy?"

"Yep. And you must be Winnie." Andy returned her handshake. "I must admit that I expected somebody older."

"Well, thanks for agreeing to meet me."

"Hey, offer me a free meal and I'll show up almost anywhere! So, what did you want to see me about?"

"Some friends and I are trying to figure out what happened to Sheriff Smitty last night."

"I've heard about you guys. The Last Chance Detectives, right?"

"Yeah, that's us."

"You guys have made the papers a few times. Solved some pretty big mysteries. And you're only kids. That's pretty cool."

"Thank you." Winnie pulled out her sketch pad and prepared to take notes. "I heard you saw a suspicious-looking car up at Suicide Curve last night. Can you tell me about it?"

"Well, we had Smitty on a gurney and were just sliding him into the back of the ambulance when I heard a car slowly approaching. You couldn't ignore it because it was really loud—in a good way. You know what I mean?"

"I guess so." Winnie didn't really know much about cars.

"Now, I kinda have a photographic memory, especially when it comes to cars. I just love vintage cars!"

"Go on," Winnie encouraged.

"Well, the one I saw last night happened to be a black 1950

Buick Roadmaster in perfect condition. Only this car's engine was definitely not stock. Somebody did some sweet aftermarket work, because the 1950 Roadmaster originally came with an overhead valve straight eight. This one sounded more like a 454 breathing through some glass packs."

"Was it dented on one side like it may have sideswiped another car?" Winnie asked.

Andy thought about it for a second. "No, it looked mint to me. Of course I didn't see the far side of the car."

"Right . . ." Winnie made a note in her sketchbook.

"But when he drove past, there was something about the way he stared at us. It definitely wasn't good."

"Wait a minute . . ." Winnie looked up from her sketchbook. "You saw his face?"

"Sure did. He drove by real slow and had his window wide open. I got a real good look at him."

"Can you describe him in detail?"

"Sure. Like I said, I have a bit of a photographic memory."

Winnie turned to a fresh page in her sketchbook and held her pencil ready. "Take your time and tell me every detail you can remember."

◆ ◆ ◆

Ambrosia's Carnegie Public Library was built in the town's heyday. It was a beautiful, neoclassical building with two main floors and a basement. Spence loved spending time within its quiet halls. He never got tired of savoring the earthy, vanilla-like odor of old books.

Tasked with finding out as much as he could about Jimmy

Sutton, Spence started his research in the basement of the library where the microfilm records were kept. His first stop was the librarian's desk.

"Excuse me, I'd like to take a look at some of your microfilm records."

A gray-haired librarian set down the book she was reading and peered over the counter.

"Microfilm? I'm surprised that a young man your age even knows what microfilm is."

Spence adjusted his glasses. "Microfilm is a film reel bearing miniature photographic copies of historical records such as legal documents, blueprints, and newspapers for archival purposes."

"Impressive," the librarian whispered. "What would you like to view?"

"I'm interested in seeing any reels you have of *The Ambrosia Signal* from June 1965 through August of that same year."

The librarian walked over to a metal cabinet and slid open one of its drawers. "Hmm. 1965, you say?"

"Correct. 1965."

The librarian looked down in the drawer and shook her head. "That's what I was afraid of."

"What's the matter?" Spence asked.

"They had a small fire at *The Ambrosia Signal* around that time." She slid the drawer closed. "I'm afraid most of the newspaper records for that year were lost."

"That's unfortunate," Spence said. "Well, thank you, ma'am."

"You're quite welcome." The librarian went back to reading her book.

Undeterred, Spence headed up to the stacks on the top floor

of the library. He knew it was quite common for most libraries to archive at least one copy of each of the local high school yearbooks. Spence was pleased to find a complete set of Ambrosia High School's yearbooks, dating back to 1921.

The date on Jimmy Sutton's tombstone revealed that he was nineteen years old at the time of his death. Spence pulled out the 1964 yearbook and turned to the back index. His eyes scanned the page and stopped on "James Sutton." Next to his name was a list of the yearbook pages that featured his picture.

The first photo was his formal senior picture. Jimmy was a good-looking young man with intense eyes, a rascally smile, and blond, slicked-back hair. In the picture, he looked unnaturally posed and uncomfortable in his dress suit.

His next appearance was a photo on a page about the Auto Shop Car Club. Spence noticed that Jimmy looked much more relaxed in this picture. Wearing a white T-shirt and cuffed blue jeans, he stood next to a black Buick Roadmaster. He was clearly mugging for the camera with his arms lazily hanging around two friends.

Spence removed a magnifying glass from his shirt pocket so he could study each of the faces in the picture. Jimmy's right arm was around a pretty girl about his same age. She was laughing and seemed to be having a great time. Sutton's left arm was around a tall, lanky young man who was making a goofy face. Spence wasn't quite sure, but something about the other boy's face looked familiar.

He glanced down to the caption below the picture and read the name of each person. Spence's face froze in astonishment.

"Incredible!" he said out loud.

Chapter 8

THE NEXT MORNING the kids met inside the B-17 to share what they had learned. They huddled around the card table and stared at the yearbook Spence had checked out of the library.

"James Sutton is in pictures throughout the yearbook," Spence explained, "but this is probably the best one—his senior picture."

Winnie looked closely at the photo. "Okay, this is getting weird."

"What do you mean?" Ben asked.

"The paramedic I interviewed told me that he not only saw a 1950 Buick Roadmaster, but he also got a good look at the driver."

Mike looked up from the photo. "He did?"

"Yeah, so I had him describe the man, and I drew a composite sketch." Winnie opened her sketch pad and set it down next to the yearbook photo. "Check it out!"

The face in the yearbook photo and Winnie's sketch were almost identical.

"A dead ringer!" Mike exclaimed. "It looks like the same guy. But how is that possible?"

"Here's another picture of him." Spence turned to the photo featuring Jimmy mugging with his two friends. "In this shot, we get a good look at his infamous car as well."

"Hold everything," Ben said. "Look at that, Mike!"

"What is it?" Winnie asked.

"Show 'em, Mike," Ben said.

"When Ben and I were out on highway 191, we found a spot in the road where it appears Smitty must've collided with another car. And we found this!" Mike placed the license plate on the card table next to the picture. "The numbers perfectly match the car in that picture!"

"This is more than weird," Winnie said. "It's getting downright spooky!"

"Then get ready to have your minds blown," Spence warned. "Check out the names under the picture of Jimmy Sutton with his friends."

Mike began reading out loud: "James Sutton makes a pit stop with his friends Donna Cooper and . . . *Theodore Smitty*!"

"*Whoa!*" the group exclaimed together.

"So, Sheriff Smitty actually knew him!" Winnie gasped.

"Not only knew him; they were friends," Spence said. "I looked up all of Smitty's high school pictures too. And in a lot of them, Jimmy is pictured either with him or in the background.

It's common to see that girl with them too. Apparently, the three of them were very good friends."

Winnie peered at the girl in the picture. "She's pretty. I wonder if she was Jimmy Sutton's girlfriend."

"Or maybe Smitty's." Spence flipped to another picture in the yearbook. "There's a photo in here of Smitty and her at some kind of school dance."

"Interesting." Winnie pulled out a sack lunch and started to arrange the contents on the card table. "What was her name again?"

"Donna Cooper," Ben replied, hungrily eyeing Winnie's lunch.

"Well, if Smitty's not willing to talk, maybe she can shed some light on this case." Winnie neatly laid out a sandwich, celery sticks, and a bag of chips. "*If* she still lives in this area, that is."

"That's a great idea, Winnie," Mike said.

"Of course, if she married she would probably have a new last name," Winnie added, eyeing Ben suspiciously. "Don't you agree, Ben?"

"Yeah," Ben mumbled, practically drooling over the food.

"Listen, guys," Winnie said as she headed to the door. "I'm gonna get a smoothie from the diner. Anybody need anything?"

"No, thanks." Mike was still engrossed with the pictures in the yearbook.

"I'll be right back." Winnie's eyes narrowed as she looked at her lunch and then at Ben. "Don't even think about it!"

Ben shook his head like that was the furthest thing from his mind. But as soon as Winnie was gone, he resumed staring at her lunch.

"How do we find this Donna Cooper, Spence?" Mike asked.

"Let's start with the most obvious way." Spence pulled a phone book off a nearby shelf and started flipping through it. "Let our fingers do the walking."

◆ ◆ ◆

Ben's empty stomach growled as he studied Winnie's lunch. It looked to be a ham sandwich. Probably delicious. He wondered if Winnie would miss one small bite, then quickly decided it would be a bad idea.

"Hey, have you guys got anything to eat?" Ben asked.

"Nope." Mike looked up from where he and Spence were flipping through the phone book. "You didn't bring your backpack full of candy?"

"No," Ben admitted. "It got so hot on our bike ride yesterday that by the time I got home, everything was melted together into one big lump. My mom made me throw it all out before I ruined the carpet."

"That's too bad." Mike went back to examining the phone book over Spence's shoulder. "See anybody named Donna Cooper in there?"

"Sorry," Spence replied.

Ben gazed miserably at the sandwich. The bread looked so fluffy and moist; he guessed that the ham inside was probably smoked. A layer of cheese made the sandwich even more tempting. His stomach let out another growl as he struggled to control himself. His head began to swim, and he broke out in a sweat.

"Hey, Ben," Mike said. "Are you feeling all right? You don't look so good."

"I'm not sure," Ben replied.

"You're not hypoglycemic, are you?" Spence asked.

Ben wiped the sweat from his forehead. "What does *hi-ho-glycemic* mean?"

"*Hypoglycemic*," Spence corrected. "Hypoglycemia is a medical condition where you need to eat at regular intervals or your blood sugar will drop."

Ben nodded. "Yeah, I think I have that."

"I'm sure your doctor would have told you by now if you really did. But it's nothing to fool around with. Hypoglycemia can cause you to pass out or even lead to death."

"So—if I had it—I'd need to eat." Ben stared at the sandwich. "Right?"

"Right."

"It might be a matter of life or death."

"Absolutely."

Ben dove for the sandwich and within a matter of seconds had ravenously consumed almost half of it. At that very moment, Winnie walked back in, carrying her smoothie. Ben's cheeks were bulging with a half-eaten sandwich when their eyes met. A look of guilt swept over his face.

"I *had* to do it!" he mumbled through an overstuffed mouthful of sandwich. "It was a matter of life and death!"

Winnie calmly walked over and sat down beside him without saying anything.

"You're not mad?" Ben asked, spraying crumbs all over her.

"Nah." Winnie shook her head and opened her bag of chips. "Go ahead. I never liked the 'Early Bird Special' anyway."

Ben's chewing slowed, and he got a funny look on his face. "Early Bird Special?"

"Yeah." Winnie patted him on the shoulder. "You know, as in 'The early bird always gets the worm!'"

Ben studied her face intently. She coyly smiled back and gave him a wink.

He finished swallowing a huge lump of food that was already halfway down his throat. A panicked look came over his face as he glanced down at the sandwich.

Under the lettuce—between the cheese and ham—a layer of wiggling worms seemed to be waving at him.

"Mealworms are actually a good source of high protein," Winnie said with a smile. "Not only are they safe to eat, but many cultures consider them a delicacy."

Ben's face turned red, and it looked like the top of his head might explode. He let out an indescribable groan and suddenly lurched forward. He slapped his hand over his mouth just as his cheeks burst full.

"No, Ben, no!" Mike could guess what was about to happen and tried to clear a path to the door. "Outside, Ben! Not in here! *Not in here!*"

Though he gave it a valiant try, Ben didn't make it to the door. The *Lady Liberty* would never be quite the same.

Chapter 9

When Spence couldn't locate Donna Cooper's name in the local phone book, Mike came up with the idea of calling the Ambrosia High School Alumni Association. The elderly man who answered the phone was a little hard of hearing but still quite helpful. Although he had no phone number for a "Donna Cooper," he did have her mailing address on record.

Wasting no time, the four kid detectives pedaled their bikes to the address, located in the Mesa Verde Trailer Park located on the far north side of town. They parked their bikes on the gravel walk in front of a modest yellow mobile home. Bowls of colorful carnations and ferns hung about the porch. An American flag flapped lazily in the wind next to a sign that read: "Sunshine Day Care."

"A babysitting place?" Ben asked. "Are you sure this is the right address, Mike?"

Mike confirmed the address he'd written down. "This should be it. Let's knock on the door and see who answers."

Ben started forward, but Winnie caught him by the elbow. "Hold on a second, Ben."

"What's up?"

Winnie squinted her eyes as she closely examined his face. "I think you've still got something stuck in between your teeth."

"Winnie!" Ben's face flushed red with anger. He started after her, but she was too fast and ran away giggling.

"Knock it off, guys," Mike said to them. "Spence and I are running out of patience. This feud of yours is getting in the way of our work!"

"Mike's right," Spence agreed and pointed at the mobile home. "What if someone is in there watching all of this? You're making us look very unprofessional."

"I'm trying not to!" Ben pointed an accusing finger at Winnie. "But she won't stop teasing me!"

"Okay, truce!" Winnie tried to put on a more serious face. "Sorry, Mike. You're right."

"How about you, Ben?" Mike asked.

"Oh, all right! Truce," Ben reluctantly agreed. "But just you wait, Winnie."

"Enough!" Mike exclaimed. "It was kind of funny at first, but this thing has gotten way out of hand." He walked up to the mobile home and knocked on the door. "You both need to put your differences aside and try to get along."

It was only a moment before the door opened. A woman stood behind the screen door, holding a crying baby.

"Yes?" The woman sounded tired.

"Pardon us, ma'am," Mike said. "I'm Mike Fowler, and this is Winnie, Ben, and Spence. We're looking for Donna Cooper."

"That would be me." She gave the infant a pacifier, and the baby quickly settled down. "What's this all about?"

"Ma'am, did you graduate from Ambrosia High?" Spence asked. "Class of 1964?"

"You can call me Donna," she said, "and, yes, I did graduate from the class of '64. Is this some sort of fundraiser for the school?"

"No, ma'am, nothing like that," Mike replied. "The four of us run the Last Chance Detective Agency."

"Maybe you've heard of us?" Ben asked.

Donna thought a second. "Yeah, I may have read something about you kids in the newspaper. Is that why you're here? Are you on a case?"

"As a matter of fact, yes," Winnie said. "We share a mutual friend with you—someone we think might be in some trouble. We hoped you might be able to help."

"Someone I know is in trouble?" Suddenly concerned, Donna stepped from behind the screen door and out onto the front porch. Though she was now in her fifties, she retained much of the beauty of her youth. "I'll try to help in whatever way I can."

"We just need to ask you a few questions," Spence said.

"No problem." Donna sat down in a wicker chair and gave them her full attention. "But first tell me who we're talking about. And what kind of trouble they're in."

"It's Sheriff Smitty, ma'am. You see, he—"

"Smitty?" Donna said flatly. The warmth and concern in her face suddenly vanished. "I see."

"Is something wrong?" Winnie asked.

"He put you up to this, didn't he?" Donna quickly stood to her feet. The baby in her arms began to cry again.

"Smitty? No. Why would he?" Ben asked.

"By now you'd think he'd at least be able to show up here himself," Donna said bitterly as she moved back toward the door.

"Smitty didn't put us up to anything," Winnie explained. "He doesn't even know we're here. We came because we wanted to ask you some questions about his friend James Sutton."

Donna paused at the front door. She turned to look at them. "What do you want to know about Jimmy?"

"We found out that the three of you had been good friends," Mike explained, "and we hoped you might be able to tell us about him."

"What do you want to know?" Donna sounded impatient.

Mike continued, "Specifically, what can you tell us about the night of July 18, 1965? Were you there?"

"Yes, I was there." Donna took a deep breath. "I suppose you want to know about how Jimmy was killed in that stupid race out at Suicide Curve."

"It's kind of important to our investigation," Ben said. "You see, there have been some reports of a—"

"Ghost car," she interrupted, finishing his sentence. "And you kids believe it?"

"No, not in ghosts," Mike assured her. "But a lot of people have seen *something*. And we were wondering: Is it at all possible that Jimmy Sutton somehow, you know, may have survived?"

Donna just stared at them for a moment. "Why don't you ask Smitty?"

"Well, we've already tried that," Winnie began. "And he . . ."

"Wait a minute," Mike said. "Are you saying that Smitty was *there* the night Jimmy died?"

"Was he *there*?" Donna shook her head in disgust. The kids could still make out her words as the screen door closed behind her: "Smitty was driving the other car!"

Chapter 10

SMITTY WAS IN HIS HOSPITAL BED, gazing out the window with a haunted expression on his face. Mike, Winnie, Ben, and Spence sat quietly in chairs around the bed. They had just revealed their discovery that he had been racing Jimmy Sutton the night of the accident. They now awaited Smitty's response.

"When I was a young man, I made some very foolish mistakes," Smitty admitted. "I haven't spoken much about what happened that night. Not because I'm trying to hide something; it's simply that I'm . . . ashamed. How did you kids find out about it?"

Mike spoke for the group: "We thought since you were laid up in the hospital we'd do a little investigating, and that led us to Donna Cooper."

"Donna—you spoke to Donna?" The kids had Smitty's full attention. "What did she have to say?"

"Only that you were the other driver," Mike said, "and that we should ask you what happened."

"She seemed kind of upset when we mentioned your name," Winnie added. "What's the deal between you two?"

"It's a long story," Smitty began, "one that goes all the way back to when I was a freshman in high school."

"We'd like to hear it," Winnie said.

"Well, our school had a bully—as most schools do, I guess. His name was Billy Clark. He was probably twenty years old but still in high school; I assume because he was held back on account of his grades. Billy had a bad temper and was as big as he was mean. The rumor was that he'd been kicked out of his previous school because he hurt somebody pretty bad. Then one day I saw him in a stairwell giving this poor freshman girl a hard time."

"Donna?" Winnie guessed.

"Yep. But I didn't know her at the time. Anyway, he's got her up against the wall, and he's teasing her while trying to kiss her. He was saying some real nasty stuff. Lots of people were standing around, but nobody was doing anything to help her. So that's when I stepped in."

"And you saved her?" Ben said.

Smitty shook his head. "I got my tail kicked. Pretty badly. I guess Billy had never been challenged like that before, because he completely lost control. After giving me a brutal whipping, he pulled out a knife."

"He had a knife in *school*?" Spence asked.

"I was helpless on the floor, and there was no doubt in my mind that he was gonna use it on me," Smitty said. "But right at that moment, this scrawny freshman emerges out of the crowd and leaps on Billy's back. It was Jimmy Sutton. I'd seen him around school before but didn't really know him."

"What happened?" Winnie asked.

"Jimmy was too small back then to really hurt Billy, but the distraction gave me time to get to my feet," Smitty explained. "I was so chock-full of adrenaline that the only thing I could do was try to knock the knife out of Billy's hand. But he bent over to throw Jimmy off his back just as my fist swung forward, and I hit him square on the chin. Nothing but dumb luck! Billy must've had a glass jaw, because he dropped the knife and collapsed just as some teachers ran up."

"Wow!" Ben exclaimed.

"The three of us—Donna, Jimmy, and myself—became really close friends from that day forward. Going through something that intense has a way of bonding people together, you know what I mean?"

"We sure do," Mike said, thinking back on all of the Last Chance Detectives' adventures together.

"There couldn't have been three more different people. Donna was reserved and kind. Jimmy was loud and impulsive, like he always had a chip on his shoulder. Guess that's why he jumped on Billy's back that day. Anyway, the three of us were inseparable throughout our four years of high school. Tried to take the same classes together. Always hung out together."

"What went wrong?" Winnie asked. "If you don't mind me asking."

Smitty looked back out the window, deep in thought. "It was the night of our senior prom," he recounted. "I can remember it like it was yesterday . . ."

Ambrosia High School Prom—1964

"Hey, Smitty!" Jimmy Sutton yelled as he made his way through the crowd gathered in the balloon-decorated gymnasium. "Couldn't you find a smaller monkey suit?"

"Thanks, pal!" an eighteen-year-old Smitty called back. He hadn't filled out yet, and his rented tux was indeed much too big for his gangly frame. He ran a comb through his slicked-back hair. "I happen to think I look pretty good!"

"Oh, yeah?" Jimmy reached up and straightened Smitty's collar. "What's the matter? Didn't anyone ever teach you how to correctly knot a bow tie?"

"What's wrong with my bow tie?" Smitty looked down just as Jimmy's finger came up and lightly tapped him on the nose.

"Gotcha!" Jimmy laughed.

"All right, wise guy!" Smitty looked around the dance floor. "Say, where's Donna?"

"Don't worry. She said she'd meet us here. Aren't you glad we all decided to go stag? This way we can dance with whoever we want." Jimmy made sure the coast was clear before reaching into his jacket pocket. "Check this out!"

"Oh, no . . ." Smitty was afraid to look. "What are you up to this time?"

"For later!" Jimmy showed Smitty a string of firecrackers, which he quickly stashed back in his pocket. "It'll help liven up the dance floor, if you know what I mean!"

"I don't think that's such a good idea—" Smitty began.

"Sutton!" The voice came from just a few yards away.

Jimmy's face fell as an older, stern-looking woman marched up to him.

"Principal Harris," Jimmy replied awkwardly. "How nice to see you."

"What was that in your pocket?" she demanded.

"In *this* pocket?" Jimmy tried to direct her to another pocket in his jacket.

"You know which pocket I mean. This one!" She pulled the string of firecrackers out of his jacket and dangled them in front of his nose.

"What?" Jimmy feigned surprise. "How did that—? This is a rented jacket! Somebody must've left them in there!"

"Your evening is over, young man!" Principal Harris grabbed Jimmy by the left ear and marched him toward the gymnasium exit. "Out you go!"

"Ow!" Jimmy protested. "I think I can hear cartilage tearing!"

As Smitty watched Jimmy's involuntary departure, he felt a tug on his left sleeve.

"What happened to Jimmy?" a female voice asked.

"Oh, Jimmy just got thrown out for . . ." Smitty's words trailed off as he turned to look at his friend. "*Donna?*"

Though Smitty had known Donna for almost four years now, he almost didn't recognize her. She usually dressed in baggy sweaters, blue jeans, and no makeup—her hair pulled back into a simple ponytail. But tonight she wore a light blue strapless chiffon dress, and her blonde hair cascaded over her shoulders. Smitty realized that he'd never seen Donna in makeup or heels before. Though he always thought she was attractive, tonight she was absolutely stunning!

"You're staring at me," she said with a hint of embarrassment.

"Am I?" Smitty tried to change the subject. "I don't think Jimmy's gonna be joining us anytime soon. How about some punch?"

As they made their way to the refreshment table, the sounds of music filled the gymnasium.

"Oh, Smitty, I love this song!" Donna exclaimed, pulling him toward the dance floor. "C'mon, let's dance!"

"I don't think I know this song," Smitty weakly protested.

"It's Santo and Johnny's 'Sleep Walk.' My absolute favorite!"

Now on the dance floor, Donna took Smitty's left hand in her outstretched palm and placed his other on her lower back.

"I'm afraid I'm not very good at this," Smitty whispered.

"Don't be silly," Donna assured him. "You're doing great."

"You're just being kind."

"No, I'm not," Donna said, looking directly into his eyes. "You're really quite wonderful."

Smitty wasn't sure if she was talking about his dancing or how she felt about him. They had simply been friends up to this point, but he was now feeling confused. It certainly felt like *something* had changed between them. Or maybe he just hadn't noticed it before. Rather than worry about it, Smitty decided to relax and just enjoy the night. The song, their dancing, the way Donna was looking at him—it all seemed so perfect. Smitty didn't want this moment to end. In a word, it was *magical.*

◆ ◆ ◆

Just off the dance floor was an emergency exit with a side window. Jimmy stood outside, his face pressed up against the glass. As he watched Smitty and Donna glide across the dance floor, for the first time since he'd known them both, Jimmy felt a growing pang of jealousy.

Chapter 11

The kids were so engaged with Smitty's story that they barely noticed when Nurse Burns knocked on the door of his hospital room.

"Sorry to interrupt," Nurse Burns said. She handed Smitty a glass of water and a paper cup containing two white tablets. "Time for your meds."

"When can I get out of here?" Smitty asked.

"Dr. Benson wants us to monitor you for one more night. You should be free to leave tomorrow."

"*Another* night?" Smitty groaned.

"Doctor's orders," the nurse said over her shoulder as she left the room.

The kids wanted to hear more of Smitty's story. "Did you and Donna become a couple after the dance?" Winnie asked.

"No." Smitty tossed the meds into his mouth and chased them down with the glass of water. "I got shipped off to Vietnam right after graduation. We were separated before anything could really blossom."

"Did you write each other letters?" Spence asked.

"A few at first, but my platoon was planted so deep in the jungle that we rarely got any mail." Smitty gazed back out the window. "The entire time I was over there, all I could think about was how lovely Donna looked on that dance floor. I decided that if I ever made it home, I'd tell her how I really felt. And that's where your grandfather comes in, Mike."

"Pop?" Mike asked.

"Yeah, I knew that Donna delivered fresh bread from her mom's bakery to the diner. So when I finally came home, I asked Pop if he would help me surprise her."

Last Chance Diner—1965

Nineteen-year-old Theodore Smitty peered out the venetian blinds of the Last Chance Diner. It was well after closing time, and there were no cars out front.

"Are you sure she's coming?" he asked Roy Fowler.

"Don't worry, she'll be here any minute," Roy assured him. "She always makes her delivery right about the time I'm closing up."

Smitty stepped away from the window and straightened his Marine dress uniform. "How do I look?"

Roy glanced up from the portable record player he had set up on the counter. "You look perfect. After being on the battlefield for almost a year, I can't believe you're letting something like this make you so nervous."

"When I was over there, I had a lot of time to think about this moment. What I would do. What I would say. I just don't want to blow it."

"You won't. I'm sure she'll . . ." Roy noticed a pair of headlights out front. "I think she's here!"

Smitty stepped to the center of the room as Roy dimmed the lights.

"I still don't know what I'm gonna say to her," Smitty admitted.

"Don't worry, the words will come to you." Roy stood ready at the record player. "When should I start the music?"

"Now. Start it now." Smitty took a deep breath, grabbed a white long-stemmed rose off a nearby table, and stood at attention.

The front door swung open just as Roy dropped the needle on the record player. "Sleep Walk" began to play. As Donna stepped into the room, Roy brought the lights up, and Smitty held out the white rose with a broad, proud smile on his young face.

The look on Donna's face was one of absolute surprise. She froze in the doorway, with several loaves of bread tucked under one arm. The other arm extended behind her as if she was holding on to something.

"What's goin' on in there?" a male voice asked from behind her.

Jimmy Sutton stepped out of the outer doorway and into the diner. He looked just as shocked as Donna.

"Smitty?"

Smitty's gaze dropped to Donna's side, and his heart sank. He could see that Jimmy was holding her hand—their fingers intimately intertwined.

The smile on Smitty's face melted away, and the stem of the rose snapped in his hand.

"Hold on, buddy!" Jimmy quickly released Donna's hand. "Let me explain!"

Without saying a word, the young marine abruptly turned on his spit-shined heel and let the rose fall to the floor.

"Please, Smitty," Donna pleaded. "Don't go!"

Smitty kicked the rose under a nearby table as he headed for the back door.

◆ ◆ ◆

More than thirty years later, the sadness still showed on Smitty's face.

"After I got over the initial shock of seeing them together like that, I was overwhelmed with jealousy and resentment. I felt like Jimmy had stolen something from me, and I wanted him to feel what it was like. So I challenged him to race for pink slips. Whoever won got to keep both cars. But if I had known what would happen . . ."

"What *did* happen?" Mike gently asked.

"We were running neck and neck on 191. Both unwilling to let off the throttle or give an inch," Smitty explained. "But neither of us suspected what we'd find when we came around the corner."

"What was it?" Ben asked.

"An animal. One of those wild burros was standing in the middle of the road. I veered one way, Jimmy swerved the other, and . . ." Smitty's words trailed off as he thought back on the events of that night. "I never meant to hurt him. He was my best friend."

"You couldn't have known what would happen." Winnie reached out a comforting hand. "It wasn't your fault."

"I immediately turned myself in to the sheriff. Admitted everything," Smitty told them. "He said that the most I could be cited for at the time was reckless endangerment. He thought that having to live with my conscience would be enough punishment, and he was right. Not a day goes by when I'm not haunted by the fact that if I hadn't challenged Jimmy to that stupid race, he would still be alive today. And Donna would . . ." Smitty took a deep breath before continuing, "Donna would still have a husband."

"*Husband?*" several of the kids said in unison.

"At the funeral, Donna's best friend told me that they had eloped three weeks earlier. Once I realized what I had done to her, I—" Smitty's voice cracked as he tried to hold in his emotions. "I tried to ask for forgiveness, but it must've come out all wrong. She moved away a few days later, probably to get away from me."

Mike could see the terrible sadness on the sheriff's face. "I'm sorry, Smitty. We had no idea."

"Ever since then, all I've wanted is a second chance to make it right—or at least that's what I thought until Donna moved back to Ambrosia last year. I'm ashamed to say that I still haven't found the courage to face her. I suppose it would probably cause more harm than good, because the bottom line is still the same. There's nothing I can do or say that will ever bring Jimmy back."

◆ ◆ ◆

"Well, *something* sure brought Jimmy back," Ben said as they left the hospital.

"C'mon, Ben!" Winnie looked at him crossly. "This is no time for joking!"

"I'm not!" Ben replied. "We've got a witness—that paramedic—who described Jimmy Sutton to a T!"

"And we have physical evidence," Spence added. "The license plate from Jimmy's car that was destroyed more than thirty years ago."

"Right," Ben continued. "And now we have a motive: Jimmy Sutton came back to get his revenge!"

"Well, I know there's no such thing as ghosts," Mike said. "But right now I can't think of another explanation."

"I'm worried that Smitty is too emotionally involved to be investigating this case," Winnie said. "I wish there was a way we could solve it before he's released from the hospital tomorrow."

"I've got an idea," Mike said, "but we're gonna need some outside help on this one."

Chapter 12

THE LAST CHANCE DETECTIVES met later that same afternoon inside the B-17, only this time they invited a guest to join them.

Pop Fowler looked a bit cramped sitting at the card table with the kids, but he listened intently as Mike laid out his plan.

When Mike was finished, Pop leaned back and rubbed his chin.

"Do you think it will work?" Mike asked.

"It might," Pop replied. "And I've got a few ideas of my own that I think will improve your plan."

"Sure!" Mike agreed.

"So, you're gonna help us?" Ben asked.

"Under one condition," Pop said firmly. "I don't want anyone getting hurt, so I'm in charge!"

◆ ◆ ◆

Several hours later, the four kids were busy putting their plan into action out on highway 191. For years Ben's family had rented a billboard advertising the Wig-Wam Motor Lodge on this stretch of road. Ben was now up on the billboard's catwalk, busily painting away.

Meanwhile, Winnie was helping Mike and Spence fasten two ten-foot-long boards together, end to end.

"This should reach across almost the entire road," Mike guessed.

"We still need ropes on each end so we can pull it back and forth," Spence reminded him.

Winnie examined the twenty-foot length of board they had assembled. "So, just how is this supposed to stop the phantom car?"

"We're not finished with it yet," Mike said. "Show her, Spence."

Spence pulled a handful of nails from a nearby box. "Once we drive several dozen of these through the boards, we'll have created a rudimentary—yet effective—spike strip."

"Wow," Winnie said. "That should definitely flatten his tires."

"And out here in the middle of nowhere, he's not gonna get very far on just his rims." Mike looked toward the sound of an approaching engine. "Here comes Pop!"

Pop's tow truck was hauling Smitty's still unrepaired pickup.

He pulled the rig to the side of the road and hopped out. "I can't believe I hauled Smitty's truck all the way out here again."

"Couldn't you have just driven it?" Winnie asked.

"No, the axle is too messed up. But I think it looks good enough to fool the person we're after." Pop wiped his brow with a red handkerchief. "Sure is hot. How's the plan coming together?"

"Good. We're almost finished with the spike strip." Mike glanced up at the billboard. "How's the painting going up there, Ben?"

"Almost done!" Ben called back.

"Winnie, can I borrow your sketch pad?" Pop asked. "I just need a page or two."

"Sure." Winnie handed him her sketch pad and pencil. "Please use the back pages. The front is filled with some sketches I hope to enter at the fair."

"No problem. I'll be careful," Pop assured her. He placed the sketch pad on the hood of the tow truck as the kids gathered around him. He drew a straight line down the middle of a blank page. "This is US 191 running north and south. Down here to the south is Route 66, which leads back to Ambrosia. Farther north, the highway eventually dead-ends at Jubilee." Pop drew an X in the middle of the line. "We're here, smack dab in the middle. The same place where Smitty was parked when he encountered what you kids call the phantom car."

"Seems as good a name as any," Spence said.

"We'll park Smitty's truck right here beneath the billboard—same as it was that night. Only I'll be sitting in for Smitty, wearing a cowboy hat identical to his."

"And I'll be hiding on the seat right next to you," Mike said with a grin. "Before the phantom realizes it's a trap, I'll sit up and videotape him with Spence's camera."

"My guess is that he knows the road dead-ends up at Jubilee, so he'll try to get away by heading back toward town." Pop looked at Spence. "This is where you come in, Spence. You'll be positioned south of us at the lower gate."

"What's the lower gate for?" Winnie asked.

"They close off this road sometimes because of flash floods," Mike explained.

"Spence, I'll radio you to close and lock that metal gate when he heads in your direction," Pop continued. "That way we'll have him trapped."

"Right!" Spence said.

Pop pointed back at the map. "Winnie, you and Ben will be positioned three miles north of here with our secret weapon. You will be on opposite sides of the road, each holding a rope tied to an end of the spike strip. At my command, pull the spike strip across the road. After he runs over it, you can pull it back out of the way."

"Why can't we just leave it there?" Winnie asked.

"Because other cars travel this road from time to time, and I really don't want to pay for all of their flat tires!"

"No kidding!" Mike laughed.

"But on a serious note . . ." Pop handed the sketch pad back to Winnie and looked at them intently. "I want you all to stay out of harm's way. At no time during this operation do I want you kids out on that road! Understand?"

"We understand," Mike said.

Pop called up to the billboard above. "Did you hear what I said, Ben?"

"I've been listening," Ben yelled down. "No going on the road!"

"How's the sign coming?" Pop asked.

"Just finished!" Ben climbed down the ladder and stepped back to admire his work. "What do you guys think?"

Ben had covered the billboard with a tarp. On it he had painted the words:

Meet you here at midnight|
-Smitty

"What's that line after the word *midnight* supposed to be?" Winnie asked.

"That's an exclamation point," Ben explained. "I thought it looked more dramatic that way."

"Well, you gotta put a dot under the line for it to look like an exclamation point!" Winnie pointed out.

"It's fine!" Ben countered.

"No, it's not. Fix it!"

"Why don't *you* fix it?"

"Fine!" Winnie marched to the sign and started to climb the ladder.

Mike walked up to Ben, shaking his head. "I wish you two would at least *try* to get along."

"Watch this," Ben whispered to Mike. In his hand was an almost invisible monofilament line leading to the paint bucket right above the ladder Winnie was climbing.

"Winnie!" Mike yelled. "Look out!"

It was too late. The bucket tipped forward and out poured almost a full gallon of paint.

Ben roared with laughter.

Winnie stood on the ladder, covered with paint from head to toe. Both her teeth and fists were clenched in rage. With paint slowly dripping down her face, she was too angry to even speak.

Chapter 13

THE MOON WAS FULL and the sky was clear, giving Pop a clear view of the road and surrounding landscape from the driver's seat of Smitty's truck. He adjusted the Stetson hat that was supposed to make him resemble Smitty, then glanced at his watch. "Half past midnight, Mike, and still no sign of your phantom car."

Mike yawned from his hiding place on the passenger seat. "I guess he didn't find our billboard in time. Or maybe he's suspicious."

"Why don't we give it another ten minutes before calling it a night?" Pop handed his grandson a walkie-talkie. "We should let the others know what we're thinking."

◆ ◆ ◆

Spence's assigned position at the lower gate of highway 191 was about a quarter mile south of Pop and Mike, but Spence was nowhere to be seen. The only living thing in the area was a large juniper bush standing near the open metal gate.

From deep within the bush came the sound of Mike's voice over the walkie-talkie: *"Come in, Spence. Do you see anything out there?"*

The branches of the juniper suddenly folded down. There was Spence, perched aboard a quad runner in the middle of his spring-loaded blind. He scanned the horizon with a pair of binoculars.

"Nothing to report. As far as I can tell, it's all quiet out here—except for a coyote to the east of you."

"How can you possibly see that?" Mike asked.

"I borrowed my dad's night-vision binoculars. They can pick up heat signatures from things like car engines or even small animals."

Spence's father was a geologist studying seismic activity in the area. He owned a lot of technical gear that he often let Spence borrow.

"Cool! Well, we're gonna wait another ten minutes and then wrap things up for tonight," Mike said.

"Copy that." Spence stepped on a pedal and his spring-loaded juniper branches snapped back into place.

◆ ◆ ◆

Winnie crouched on a small rise off to the side of the highway. With a small penlight clenched between her teeth, she flipped through her sketchbook and was heartbroken by what she saw. Ben's paint had seeped through the pages and destroyed most of her artwork.

"Come in, Winnie," Mike's voice came over the walkie-talkie.

"Go ahead, Mike." Her voice was a little shaky.

"You guys okay over there?" Mike asked.

"Yeah, I guess so."

"How about Ben?"

From Winnie's position she could look down at Ben across the road. He sat in a small beach chair—head tilted back, mouth wide open—fast asleep.

"He's conked out," Winnie said into her walkie-talkie.

"Well, wake him up!" Mike instructed. *"Tell him he's only got to stay awake for about ten more minutes before we pack it in for the night."*

"Roger and out." Winnie set down her walkie-talkie and cupped her hands around her mouth. "Ben!" she whispered as loud as she could.

Ben let out a snort but didn't wake.

Winnie didn't want to yell, so she tore off a scrap of paper and rolled it into a ball. She took careful aim and tossed it across the road at Ben.

She missed him by a good five feet.

Undeterred, she wadded up another paper ball and tossed it a little harder. This time she almost hit his foot.

"Just need to give it a little more *oomph,*" Winnie whispered to herself. She balled up a third piece of paper and threw it as hard as she could. It arced over the road and landed in Ben's open mouth.

Ben's eyes popped open, and he clutched at his throat. He rolled out of the chair, hacking and coughing until the ball of paper popped out. Now on all fours, he looked up at Winnie, who was covering her mouth and trying not to laugh.

"Winnie!" he croaked.

"Shh!" Winnie whispered. "Someone might hear you!"

"I don't care!" Ben said loudly. "Practically choking somebody to death is going too far!"

"I didn't mean to!" Winnie's voice level was rising as well. "Besides, you went too far when you dumped paint all over my sketches!"

Ben got to his feet and began dusting himself off. "Oh, big deal."

"Yeah, it is a big deal!" Winnie held up her paint-soaked sketchbook. "These drawings represent months of hard work. My hopes of competing in the county fair are completely destroyed thanks to you!"

"I'd feel *ever* so sorry, Winnie," Ben said sarcastically, "but it's your own fault for starting this feud in the first place!"

"*My* fault?" Winnie couldn't believe her ears. "You're saying that *I* started it?"

"That's *exactly* what I'm saying. Remember gluing my rear to that chair?"

"That's because you drew that goofy picture of me!"

"Can't you take a little joke?" Ben asked. "Boy, you're sensitive. I told Mike we should have never allowed a girl into our group."

"What?"

"You heard what I said."

Winnie looked wounded. "You don't want me to be part of the Last Chance Detectives?"

Ben just shrugged.

Winnie was hurt, and now she wanted to hurt Ben back. "That's really something coming from the one person who never—and I mean *never*—contributes anything to any of our cases."

"I do, too!"

"Really? Name something—just *one* thing you bring to the group."

Ben momentarily seemed to draw a blank. He thought for a few seconds, then said, "I'm here tonight, aren't I?"

"You were just asleep, remember?" Winnie yelled louder than she intended. Her voice echoed in the canyon.

This time it was Ben's turn to look hurt. "I can't believe you don't think I'm good for anything."

"Yeah? Well, I can't believe you didn't want me in the group."

Their painful words hung heavily in the air. Now that they'd been spoken, there was no taking them back.

◆ ◆ ◆

Pop rubbed his eyes and took off the Stetson. "Sorry, Mike. I guess it wasn't meant to be. I'll go get the tow truck so we can haul this thing back to town. You better let everyone know that we're calling it a night."

As Pop got out of Smitty's pickup, Mike sat up in his seat and fastened his seatbelt. His neck was sore from hiding in such cramped quarters for so long.

"Winnie . . . Spence . . ." he called into the walkie-talkie. "I'm afraid that's it. You can start packing things up. Pop and I will be by to pick you up in a few minutes."

"Hold on, Mike." It was Spence's voice. *"I've spotted something. . . ."*

"Is it a car coming up the highway?" Mike asked.

"Negative." There was an intensity in Spence's voice. *"I have a moving heat signature in your area."*

Mike looked around and then relaxed. "That's just Pop walking down the road to get the tow truck from where he hid it."

"It's not Pop!" Spence insisted. *"The object I'm looking at is way too big! And it's not moving away from you—it's moving toward you!"*

Mike peered out the truck's front windshield. "I don't see anything. There's nothing on the highway in either direction."

"It's not on the highway!" Spence sounded panicked. *"Whatever it is, it appears to be coming down the hill directly behind—"*

BLAM!

Smitty's truck was suddenly struck violently from behind. Mike's head whiplashed back and the walkie-talkie flew out of his hand.

Spence's frightened voice could still be heard coming from the small speaker: *"Get out of there, Mike!"*

Chapter 14

WINNIE HEARD THE DISTANT CRASH and wondered what could possibly be happening.

"Winnie!" It was Spence's voice on her walkie-talkie. *"I'm closing the gate. Move the spike strip onto the road!"*

"Roger!" Winnie waved across the road to Ben. "Here we go! Pull the spike strip out!"

"All right, all right!" Ben pulled his end of the rope, and the spike strip slid out of the bushes into the road. But in all the excitement, he pulled a little too hard, and the strip wasn't quite centered. "Winnie, bring it back a bit!"

Just as they had practiced, Winnie pulled the rope from her side of the road, and the spike strip slid back a few feet. It was now perfectly centered.

"That's good!" Ben yelled.

"We're all set, Spence!" Winnie radioed. "Is Mike okay?"

"I don't know," Spence answered.

◆ ◆ ◆

At first, Mike wasn't sure what had just happened. One moment he was talking to Spence on the radio, and the next—Smitty's truck was rammed hard from behind.

Mike guessed that it must be the phantom car. It had been hidden in the hills behind them all along. The driver must have coasted down the dirt embankment because Mike never heard the approaching sound of an engine.

Now the Buick's motor roared to life. In the truck's rearview mirror, Mike could see the headlights of the car as it backed up for several yards. To his horror, the driver gunned the engine and started forward again.

Again the truck was hit hard from behind. Only this time whoever was behind the wheel didn't let up on the gas, pushing Smitty's pickup clear across the road. Mike unbuckled his seatbelt and tried to move to the driver's seat so he could stop the truck's forward movement, but the front bumper hit the guardrail before he could apply the brakes.

Mike suddenly realized that the railing was the only thing holding him from a deadly drop into the canyon below.

The Buick backed up again, got another running start, and again smashed into the rear of the truck. The bed of the pickup buckled. Cracks appeared in the back window. The guardrail groaned as it tried to withstand the weight of the two cars. Mike knew he had to get out of the truck right away, but the driver's door wouldn't budge. He slid over to the passenger door just as the pickup was hit from behind again.

There was no doubt in Mike's mind that whoever was driving the other car was trying to kill him. The classic hot rod was now a weapon. A battering ram.

Smitty's truck was hit again—even harder this time. Mike was slammed against the dashboard. Even worse, the guardrail began to buckle. Mike knew it wouldn't hold for long. He tried the passenger door, but it was stuck as well. He was trapped inside the pickup with no way out!

The smell of burning rubber filled the night air. The Buick's wheels spun angrily as it pushed the truck against the weakened railing. In a panic, Mike tried to break the passenger window with his elbow. He hit it as hard as he could, yet the glass held firm.

The Buick backed up again, even farther this time. There was no way the guardrail could withstand another blow. Mike waved frantically out the back window.

"I'm not Smitty!" he yelled with all the volume he could muster. "I'm just a kid!"

His pleading did no good. The Buick's engine was a loud roar, drowning him out. The driver revved the motor to maximum, preparing to deliver the final, fatal blow.

"*Nooo!*" Mike screamed.

As Mike watched helplessly, everything seemed to move into slow motion. Flames shot forth from the hood portals as the Buick growled with vengeance. The next moment it was speeding straight for him! Mike could only brace for the coming impact.

The sound of the collision was even louder than he expected. But, oddly, he felt nothing.

Mike lifted his head and was shocked to see that the Buick was no longer nearby. The sound he had heard was Pop's heavy tow truck striking the Buick's passenger side door. The unexpected blow spun the black car around for a full revolution before it came to a stop about twenty yards down the road. Broken glass and pieces of chrome scattered across the highway. As the sound of the collision echoed off the distant hills, the Buick showed no signs of life—its headlights off and the engine apparently dead.

Pop was already out of the tow truck, motioning for Mike to move away from the back window of Smitty's pickup. With one blow from Pop's hammer, the already cracked window shattered, and Mike crawled out.

"Hurry, Mike!" Pop said. "Get in the truck!"

They were halfway across the road when they heard the sound of the Buick's ignition system firing. The car's headlights flickered dimly with each failed attempt to restart the engine.

Mike and Pop quickly climbed into the relative safety of the tow truck.

"Are you okay?" Pop asked.

"Mostly," Mike said, but he was clearly trembling. "You got here just in time!"

"Well, hang on!" Pop put the tow truck into gear. "We're getting out of here!"

Chapter 15

Spence had watched the entire scene play out through his binoculars. Now he was relieved to see that Pop and Mike were putting some distance between themselves and the phantom car.

Spence lowered his binoculars and lifted his walkie-talkie. "Come in, Winnie."

"Go ahead, Spence," Winnie replied.

"They're headed in your direction."

"The phantom car?"

"No, Pop and Mike. They're in the tow truck. Pull the spike strip off the road."

"Gotcha!" Winnie replied.

Spence raised his binoculars in time to see the headlamps of the Buick suddenly flash on. Even from that distance, he could hear the roar of its engine coming back to life. He watched with concern as it accelerated away in the same direction as Pop and Mike.

"Oh, no," he whispered.

◆ ◆ ◆

Winnie coiled the rope around her forearm and began pulling the spike strip off the highway.

"Hey!" Ben yelled from across the road. He quickly yanked the spike strip back to the center of the road. "What do you think you're doing?"

"I know exactly what I'm doing!" Winnie pulled the spike strip back toward her side.

"Oh yeah?" Ben gave the rope a hard tug.

"Stop it!" Winnie yanked even harder.

They both heard the sound as the rope snapped.

Ben looked at Winnie with disbelief. "I can't believe you just broke it!"

"Because you wouldn't let go!" Winnie pulled the spike strip off to her side of the road. "Spence wants it out of the road! Pop and Mike are coming!"

"Why didn't you say so?" Ben yelled.

Winnie was practically trembling with anger. "I just did!"

◆ ◆ ◆

Pop glanced in the rearview mirror and saw the headlights of the phantom car quickly gaining on them.

"Make sure you're buckled in," Pop warned Mike.

"What's the matter?" Mike asked.

Pop pointed his thumb over his shoulder. "We've got company back there!"

As Mike turned around to look, the Buick bumped up against the tow truck, pushing it into the oncoming lane.

"Oh, no!" Mike said.

"If he wants to get by on the right, then so be it! I won't put up a fight!" Pop steered the tow truck to the left and slowed down.

The Buick pulled alongside the tow truck and maintained a steady pace.

"What's with this guy?" Mike asked. "He's got to know by now that we're not Smitty."

Mike could see clearly into the Buick. A ghostly apparition stared back. It looked exactly like the photo of Jimmy Sutton from the yearbook, only it seemed to be made of transparent smoke that was constantly writhing and changing. As Mike watched, the features of Jimmy's face sank, his skin decayed, and his head became almost skeletal. The terrifying figure smiled, shook his head, and wagged his bony finger back and forth as if shaming them.

Mike was suddenly startled by a loud hiss. White-hot steam poured from the front of Pop's tow truck.

"Must've cracked the radiator when I rammed him," Pop guessed. "Look's like this is as far as we go."

"He'll get away!" Mike said hopelessly.

"We've got no choice," Pop said with a shrug.

With one last rev of the engine, the Buick accelerated past the struggling tow truck and disappeared around the corner ahead.

Pop pulled the truck to the side of the road, and Mike picked up the walkie-talkie. "Come in, Winnie."

"Go ahead, Mike."

"He's headed your way," Mike warned. "Put the spike strip back out on the road."

"You want it back *on the road?"*

"Yes, back on the road. And hurry, he's almost there!"

"Got it!" Winnie responded.

"They're about a quarter-mile up the road," Pop told Mike. "Run on ahead and I'll catch up."

"Okay!" Mike jumped out of the cab and started sprinting.

"Keep everyone safely away from him until I get there!" Pop called after him.

◆ ◆ ◆

"Ben!" Winnie yelled. "Pull the spike strip back over to your side!"

"I would," Ben yelled back, "but *somebody* broke the rope! Remember?"

Winnie tried to push the homemade spike strip out onto the road, but without Ben pulling from the other side, it slid sideways and tipped over. Winnie could see that the spikes were no longer facing up. She could also hear the distant rumble of an approaching car. Time was running out, and fast.

"Help me!" she shouted to Ben.

"I can't!" Ben yelled. "You heard what Pop said about staying off the road!"

"But he's coming! What am I supposed to do?"

"I don't know! *You* broke it—*you* fix it!"

Winnie groaned in frustration. She quickly ran onto the road, pulling the spike strip behind her.

"What are you *doing*?" Ben shouted. "Stay off the road!"

"There, it's fixed!" As Winnie turned to run to safety, her foot accidentally kicked the spike strip. The device tipped over again, and Winnie bent down again to fix it.

"Get out of there, Winnie! The car's coming!" Ben yelled.

It took Winnie only a moment to set the spike strip upright, but her heart sank as she heard the roar of the Buick's engine. She hadn't expected it to arrive so soon. Now in a panic, she tried to run for cover, but the loose gravel beneath her sneakers caused her foot to slip. She felt a deep stab of pain as her ankle twisted, then buckled. She fell hard, her chin hitting the blacktop first. Winnie desperately tried to get up, but her ankle was throbbing.

The Buick appeared around the corner, moving much too fast to stop. Winnie managed to get up on one knee, but it was too late.

"*Winnieeee!*" Ben screamed.

Chapter 16

MIKE SPRINTED DOWN THE DARK HIGHWAY with only the moon and stars to light the way. A few moments earlier he'd heard the sound of screeching tires, a low thud, and then a crash. He hoped the spike strip had worked and that everyone was okay. But as he rounded the corner, the scene was a nightmare come to life.

The Buick lay on its roof in a sea of shattered glass. It had obviously lost control and run up the dirt embankment before flipping over. One of its wheels was still slowly spinning.

In its headlights, Mike could make out two silhouettes on the road. One rocked back and forth, cradling the head of the other.

"Spence!" Mike shouted into his walkie-talkie. "We need an ambulance! Now!"

Mike ran up to the two figures, terrified of what he might find.

"Winnie!" Mike gasped. "What happened?"

Winnie looked up at Mike, tears streaming down her face. "He pushed me out of the way at the last moment."

Ben's eyes were closed, and he wasn't moving. There didn't seem to be a scrape on him, but his body was twisted in an awkward position. His face was ashen.

"Ben . . ." Mike knelt by his side. "Can you hear me? An ambulance will be here soon."

Ben's eyes fluttered open as he tried to focus on his friend. "Mike?" Ben's voice was little more than a whisper. "Did we catch him?"

Mike looked over at the smoking wreckage, then back at Ben. "I think so."

"After all I've been through," Ben tried to joke through labored breathing, "you better not let him get away . . ." Ben suddenly grimaced as a fresh wave of pain swept over him.

Mike grabbed his hand and held it tight. "He won't get away, Ben. I promise!"

Ben tried to respond, but his eyes glazed over and slowly rolled back. His body went limp.

"Ben!" Winnie cried. "Stay with us!"

Spence's quad runner rolled onto the scene, and Pop jumped off the back. He rushed over to Ben and gently pushed Mike aside.

"Give me some room to work, Mike." Pop lifted Ben's wrist and checked for a pulse. "Winnie, tell me what happened."

As Winnie began to explain, Mike stumbled backward in a state of shock. "Where's that ambulance, Spence?"

"It's on the way," Spence assured him.

Trying to make sense of what was happening, Mike nervously ran his fingers through his hair and walked toward the smoking wreckage. Through the shattered front windshield, Mike noticed the sparks of short-circuiting computer equipment. He could also see that the driver's side window had been frosted to display video from a rear-projection system. An eerily realistic image of Jimmy Sutton's "ghost" appeared on the window's cracked surface. The malfunctioning video loop ran forward, froze, stuttered for a moment, then repeated the process again.

Mike could make out shoeprints in the dirt where someone had made their escape after climbing through the broken windshield.

"I've got no pulse!" Pop's distant voice shouted.

Mike closed his eyes, wishing that it was somehow all just a bad dream.

"I'm going to start chest compressions." Pop leaned over Ben with both palms on the boy's chest. "One, two, three—"

"We'll get him, Ben," Mike said under his breath. "I promise!"

Chapter 17

JUST BEFORE DAWN, Pop and the kids huddled together in the emergency waiting room of the county hospital.

"And we thank You, dear Lord, for your great mercies," Pop prayed. "We ask, now, for a miracle—that You will give the doctors wisdom and skill. We commit Ben into Your loving hands. In Jesus' name we ask this. Amen."

Pop looked up at the kids. He could tell that they were scared. "You did well," Pop assured them. "We got him here alive. Now it's out of our hands."

Winnie could no longer hold in her anguish and sobbed loudly. "Ben, he . . . he . . ." She could barely get out the words. "He saved my life!"

Spence put his hand on her shoulder. "It's okay, Winnie."

"No, it's not!" she cried. "You don't know the horrible things I said to him—the names I called him!"

"Oh, Winnie," Pop said. "I'm sorry."

"I was so wrong to take him for granted," she cried. "I only hope it's not too late to tell him—" Winnie paused mid-sentence as Carl "Doc" Benson, Ambrosia's resident physician, entered the waiting room. He looked tired and worried as he approached the group with his usual stiff gait.

Pop stood to his feet. "What can you tell us, Doc?"

Doc Benson sat down opposite them. "Ben's family asked me to give you an update on his condition. They hoped you might pray for him."

"We have been and will continue," Pop said. "How is he?"

"He's got several broken ribs and a punctured lung. And we had to remove his spleen. But he's been stabilized for now."

"Do you think he's going to make it?" Mike asked.

Doc took a deep breath before continuing. "Although the medical team has done everything they can, the prognosis is not good. With the sort of injuries Ben sustained, it's hard to know for sure if we were able to stop all the internal bleeding. What that boy needs is a miracle."

"How's his family taking this?" Pop asked.

"Right now they're at his bedside, keeping vigil in case he doesn't pull through."

The room was silent as the sobering news sank in.

Mike suddenly stood to his feet and marched out of the waiting room. Pop quickly followed.

In the dimly lit corridor, Pop caught up with Mike near a stairwell and gently grabbed him by the shoulder. "Where are you going, Mike?"

"I don't know." Mike tried to look brave, but his eyes were filling with tears. "But I can't just sit in there and wait to see if someone else I love is taken away from me!"

"We don't know if that's going to happen," Pop said.

"No, but in the meantime whoever did this to Ben is still out there running free!" Mike wiped the tears from his eyes, and a look of anger swept over his face. "I plan to find out who it is, and to make sure he pays for it!"

"Now hold on a minute." Pop took Mike by both shoulders and looked him square in the eyes. "There's nothing wrong in seeking justice, Mike. But I'm afraid that what I see in you right now is more like a thirst for revenge."

"And what's wrong with that?" Mike asked. "I mean, what are we supposed to do? Just 'turn the other cheek' while this guy gets away scot-free? That's not right!"

"No, it's not. And we're *not* going to just let him go," Pop said firmly. "But we're also not going to give in to the very thing that caused all this pain in the first place."

"What do you mean?"

"Revenge isn't justice, Mike. It's just another word for hate," Pop explained. "It's what put Smitty in the hospital. On a smaller scale, it's why Winnie can't forgive herself. It's also why your friend in there is fighting for his life."

"Okay, but that was for the wrong reasons," Mike said in frustration. "This is a good one. I mean, look what he did to Ben!"

"God's principles—His truth—doesn't change based on the situation, even if someone's been hurt. Let me see the Bible your dad gave you."

Mike pulled out the pocket Bible he always carried and

handed it to his grandfather. Pop quickly thumbed through the pages and found the passage he was looking for.

"Never take your own revenge . . ." Pop read, ". . . for it is written: 'Vengeance is mine, I will repay,' says the Lord. 'But if your enemy is hungry, feed him; if he is thirsty, give him a drink; for in so doing you will heap burning coals on his head.' Do not be overcome by evil, but overcome evil with good."

Mike shook his head in disbelief. "What are you saying—that we should just give him his car back? Maybe pound out the dents while we're at it, and send him on his way?"

"Not at all," Pop said. "The Bible teaches that God loves justice. One of the responsibilities He gave us is to fight evil and protect the helpless. But before we confront the sinner, this passage tells us that we need to examine our own hearts. Are we acting out of love? And are we willing to forgive?"

"Forgive?" Mike took a deep breath and stared down at the floor. "I don't know if I can."

"I'm afraid I know that feeling," said a voice from behind them.

◆ ◆ ◆

Mike and Pop turned to see Donna Cooper standing nearby. Her eyes looked like she had been crying. "I didn't mean to eavesdrop," she said, "but I couldn't help but overhear what you were saying."

"Donna." Pop extended his hand. "It's good to see you."

"I heard the news and came as soon as I could," she explained.

"Thanks for coming," Pop said. "This is my grandson, Mike."

"We've met." Donna turned to Mike. "I want to apologize for not helping you when I had the chance. I'm afraid that all of this might be my fault."

"Don't worry, ma'am," Mike assured her. "We know this has nothing to do with Jimmy Sutton . . . I mean, your late husband."

"I know that too." Donna paused and a sad look came over her face. "But I'm afraid it has *everything* to do with our son."

Pop and Mike exchanged glances, wondering if they had heard her correctly.

"You see, my parents never approved that I eloped with Jimmy. Even after his death they wanted to keep it a secret, so we moved to California. But life has a way of surprising you. Six months later little JJ was born."

Donna pulled out her wallet to show them a picture. "This is him a few years back."

Pop looked at the photo. "He's the spitting image of his dad!"

"I think so too." Donna studied the picture and reflected. "He's a little older than his father in this photo, and maybe a little angrier. But I suppose that's my fault."

"Your fault?" Mike asked.

"For a long time I was very angry," Donna said. "Angry that I lost my husband. Angry that JJ had to grow up without a father. I foolishly needed someone to blame it on, so I directed my anger toward Smitty. When JJ was old enough to ask what happened to his father, I wanted him to be proud. In the version of the story that I told, his daddy was the hero and Smitty was, well, I guess he was the villain. Over time, even I started to believe that version."

"Donna, it was an accident," Pop said. "Smitty wasn't at fault."

"Deep down I've always known that's true," Donna confessed. "But by the time I was willing to admit it to JJ, the lie had taken its toll. He was obsessed with getting even."

"Oh, no," Pop said sadly.

"Unfortunately, no matter how many times I've tried to set the record straight, JJ still blames Smitty." Donna began to cry. "When I heard about the phantom car, I told myself that it couldn't be JJ, that he wouldn't go that far. But when he came by my house a few hours ago, I realized the horrible truth."

"What happened?" Pop asked. "What did JJ tell you?"

"He showed up all cut and bruised, as if he'd been in an accident. He was panicked. Said he accidentally hit a kid." Donna shook her head in shame. "That's why I came to the hospital—to talk to Smitty."

"You spoke with Smitty?" Mike asked.

"Ironic, isn't it? After all these years, I was the one who needed to apologize." Donna pulled a handkerchief from her purse and wiped her eyes. "I was wrong to blame him all this time. And now that the tables are turned, I understand what he must have been going through. That's why I told him where I think JJ is hiding out."

"Donna, I'm so glad you came here to do what's right," Pop said. "But I'm concerned that Smitty's emotional and personal involvement in this situation might cloud his judgment. I'm going to advise Smitty that he allow someone else to be the arresting officer."

"I'm afraid it might be too late for that," Donna explained.

"He had just checked himself out of the hospital when I left him."

"Donna, can you tell me where Smitty was headed?" There was an urgency in Pop's voice. "Where do you think your son is?"

"JJ is the caretaker of the old ghost town."

"Jubilee?"

"Yes. The movie studios hired him to watch over the equipment and sets they've stored up there."

"How long ago did Smitty leave?" Pop asked.

"Probably about fifteen minutes ago."

"Thank you, Donna." Pop headed for the hospital exit. "Mike, get Spence. I'll pull my car around front."

"Maybe I should go with you," Donna called after him.

"I think you should stay here with Winnie." Pop paused at the exit. "But please pray."

"I will," she assured him. "I think we could all use a miracle about now."

Chapter 18

THE GHOST TOWN OF JUBILEE was located nearly 2,000 feet above Ambrosia, where US 191 finally came to an end. It began as a small mining camp in 1883, when two prospectors discovered a vein of gold worth several million dollars. Within a year Jubilee's population had exploded to well over 3,000 people. Hotels, mercantile stores, and saloons were hastily built to satisfy the needs and wants of its new citizens. A few miners made a fortune, while others lost everything. Yet within a decade the mines had all run dry. Just as quickly as it had grown, Jubilee was soon abandoned.

Because of the preserving nature of the desert and the town's relatively remote location, most of Jubilee's vacated buildings still stood—though now very worn and sun-bleached. There were fifty-eight vintage structures in all, including a once-operational gold mill. Many of the interiors remained as they once were, some still stocked with tools and other goods.

Movie production companies used the location when they needed to film in an authentic Western town. They added a few buildings over the years and outfitted many of them with props. They even constructed a replica train station; though, in reality, the miners of Jubilee used burros to carry out their ore in the 1800s.

The Wild West ghost town now represented quite an investment. Since it was also deemed a historic site, Jubilee's preservation became a concern. A security fence was erected around the perimeter, and a caretaker was hired to chase off vagrants, vandals, and anyone who might steal equipment from the property. That caretaker was the young Jimmy Sutton.

As the morning sun appeared in the distant hills, Sheriff Smitty parked his Crown Victoria sedan outside the security fence and limped up to the main gate. His injured ankle was secure inside a walking boot, but it still hurt to put his full weight on it.

Dressed in his sheriff's uniform, Smitty pressed the call button on a metal security box and flashed his badge at an overhead closed-circuit camera. He waited several minutes, but no one answered. He pressed the call button a few more times and waited. No response.

Smitty noticed that the front gate had no padlock, so he gave it a push. With a loud creak, the gate swung wide open.

Smitty stepped back and looked up at the security camera. "This is Sheriff Theodore Smitty!" he called out. "I'm coming in on official business!"

Still no answer.

Smitty hobbled through the open gate. He wondered if it was a simple oversight, or if it had been left unlocked on purpose. Either way, he had the feeling that he was being watched.

◆ ◆ ◆

The desert winds that blew through the canyons were usually stronger at the higher elevation, but Smitty wondered if an approaching storm was making them blow especially hard this morning.

Smitty stepped onto the ghost town's main street. An old windmill missing some of its blades still noisily turned. The wind almost blew off Smitty's hat as the growing gusts made an eerie howling noise that sent a shiver down his spine.

He cupped his hands to his mouth and shouted: "JJ Sutton, this is Sheriff Smitty! If you can hear my voice, please come out so we can talk!"

The sheriff's voice bounced off the buildings at the end of the street and echoed back at him. For a moment Smitty thought he saw some movement in a second-story window, but a closer inspection revealed that it was just an old lace curtain blowing in the wind.

"JJ!" Smitty shouted. "Your mom, Donna, told me that I would find you here! She also told me what happened! We need to talk!"

Smitty listened for a response and heard a rhythmic banging noise coming from the nearby livery stable. He slowly limped to the open doorway, half expecting to see a blacksmith hammering a horseshoe into shape. Instead, he found a heavy chain swinging in the wind against a rusted anvil.

Smitty stepped back out into the street. "Don't be afraid, JJ! I know you didn't mean to hit the boy! We can work it out, son!"

Still no response.

His ears picked up on the sound of approaching steps. Walking cautiously toward the sound, Smitty discovered a wild burro rounding a nearby corner. He knew that the animals were often seen roaming the hills around Jubilee. They were direct descendants of the animals used to haul ore out of town. Smitty wondered if this was somehow the very same one that wandered onto the highway the day of that fateful accident.

The burro paused to momentarily look him over, then continued on its way.

Smitty wondered what other surprises awaited him.

Chapter 19

THE TIRES ON POP FOWLER'S CAR SQUEALED as they hugged a sharp turn on highway 191. Pop was eager to get to Jubilee, but he also knew he needed to get there safely. He, Mike, and Spence had been up for more than twenty-four hours and were completely exhausted.

"I sure could use some coffee," Pop said. "We probably should have picked up some breakfast before we left town, but we don't have any time to spare."

"I'm not hungry." Mike stared at the road ahead. "I keep thinking about Ben."

"Me, too," said Spence from the back seat.

"Ben is in God's hands now," Pop told them. "And He's a God of miracles. That's not to say He always answers our prayers just the way we want. But we can rest assured that He loves Ben and is working out His perfect plan."

Neither Mike nor Spence responded. The trio was quiet for the next several miles.

Pop finally broke the silence. "Did either of you bring your walkie-talkie?"

"I did," Spence replied.

"Can you reach the sheriff's office from out here?"

"Probably," Spence guessed. "I think Arlene monitors the emergency channel."

"If you don't mind me using it, I'd like to try to contact her before we get out of range."

"Sure." Spence handed his walkie-talkie to Pop. "Go ahead. You should be all set."

Pop kept one hand on the wheel while he began transmitting. "Come in, Arlene. This is Pop Fowler. Do you copy?"

"This is Arlene. Go ahead, Pop."

"Arlene, I'm driving up to Jubilee and want to check in with you before I get out of range. We heard that Smitty was headed up that way. Do you know if that's true? Over."

"Yes, he last reported in about twenty minutes ago, just before he got there. But I haven't been able to reach him since. Over."

"That's because those rocky canyons can interfere with radio signals. Over."

"That's probably it. But I'm so glad you radioed me, Pop. If you see Smitty, I need you to pass on a piece of information for me. Over."

"I can do that, Arlene. What is it? Over."

"Tell him that the charges against the man he's after just went up to manslaughter. Over."

"Manslaughter? For what?"

"Oh, Pop, I hate to tell you this way . . ." Arlene sounded on the verge of tears. *"But I just got word that Ben Jones didn't make it."*

"Come again?" Pop hoped he had misunderstood her.

"Ben didn't make it. I'm so sorry, Pop. Over."

"Arlene, I, uh . . ." Pop's voice cracked, and he stared numbly out the windshield. "I'll pass on the information. Over."

"No!" Spence gasped.

Mike pounded the seat as hard as he could.

Pop's heart broke.

◆ ◆ ◆

Smitty limped down the deserted streets, searching the rustic buildings for any sign of life. He still had the distinct impression that he was being watched.

"I'm not going away, JJ!" Smitty shouted. "Come out from wherever you're hiding so that we can straighten this thing out!"

Smitty listened intently. The wind continued to howl. The buildings around him creaked. In the distance, a shutter banged against its splintered window frame. If JJ was nearby, he was certainly keeping quiet.

Then Smitty *did* hear something: music. It was faint at first, but it sounded like someone was playing a piano in the saloon at the end of the street. As Smitty got closer, he could tell that it was a lively tune. Yes, he distinctly recognized a ragtime version of "Camptown Races." He could also make out voices. They were quite loud and jovial, as if a party was going on inside.

Smitty looked up at the sign over the door: "The Kicking Mule Saloon." As he hobbled up the steps, he wondered if a production crew might be inside—possibly celebrating the end of a long film shoot. But that was unlikely. He surely would have seen their vehicles.

Everything went quiet the moment Smitty pushed open the saloon's swinging café doors. The sounds of music faintly echoed in the large room, but the piano bench was empty. Drinking glasses and cards lay scattered on the tables, and a thin layer of what smelled like cigar smoke hung in the air above empty chairs. A colorful roulette wheel at the far side of the room slowly spun to a stop. It was like a scene from a Wild West movie: everyone in the saloon was having a great time, at least until the sheriff arrived. Only this time, when the lawman showed up, everybody vanished.

Smitty knew he wasn't crazy, but he wondered what had become of the people he'd heard. He checked under the tables and behind the bar. No one in sight. Had someone lured him in, perhaps using prerecorded voices and hidden speakers?

He decided that he'd better get outside fast.

Smitty turned toward the entrance, but it was already too late.

The building trembled, and Smitty heard the sound of metal sliding down and slamming into place. A quick glance around the room revealed that all the doors and windows were now covered with bars like a jail cell.

Smitty tried not to panic. With both hands, he grabbed the bars blocking the front doors. Perhaps the bars might slide back the way they came. But try as he might to move them, they wouldn't budge an inch. The bars were made of thick, case-hardened steel, so bending them was also out of the question.

He was trapped.

Chapter 20

Pop recognized that no one in the car had said a word for the last several miles—not since they had received the news about Ben. Turning to look at Spence, he saw that the boy was bent over with his face in his hands. Pop guessed he was probably crying. But it was Mike he was more worried about. His grandson just stared out the passenger window in silence—a tightly clenched fist slowly punching the armrest.

"We're all hurting right now," Pop finally said. "But, Mike, I want you to remember what we talked about earlier."

Mike continued to stare out the window.

"I know you're upset right now. But don't be overcome with anger."

"He killed Ben!"

"That doesn't change how we're supposed to respond . . ."

"It changes *everything*!" Mike said loudly. "How can you just sit there and not be upset?"

Pop let the question hang in the air for nearly a minute.

"I *am* upset," Pop finally said. "You have no idea. I'm mostly upset with myself for taking you kids out there in the first place. Talk about a foolish thing to do! I would change places with Ben if I could."

Pop hoped Mike could see that he was hurting just as much as his grandson.

"The sad truth is that the older you get in life, the more you realize just how many mistakes you've made," Pop admitted. "Mistakes that will haunt you for years. And you'll wish so hard that you could somehow take them back. But there are no do-overs."

Pop slowed the car as they passed a sign welcoming them to historic Jubilee.

"The only comfort I can find is that I've been forgiven," he said. "In the end, I'm going to stand before God and *not* get what I deserve. It's called grace. And I'm so thankful for that—so thankful I've been forgiven that I can't help but extend the same forgiveness to others."

Mike pointed out the front windshield. "There's Smitty's car!"

"Okay, we're here to simply back up Smitty," Pop reminded the boys as he parked the vehicle. "I'm also hoping that our presence here might keep things calm."

◆ ◆ ◆

Smitty hurriedly examined every corner of the Kicking Mule Saloon, searching for any way out. All the windows and doors were completely barred over. He could see a second-story landing, but no stairway leading up to it.

He wondered if he might be able to reach the landing if he stood on a table and leaped as high as he could. But he would still have to pull himself up and over the second-story railing. In his banged-up condition—with a bruised shoulder and his foot in a heavy walking boot—pulling off that sort of maneuver was virtually impossible.

"Theodore Smitty!" called a voice from above.

Smitty turned to see JJ Sutton looking down at him from the second-story landing. He was the spitting image of his father. The same height and build. The same slicked-back blond hair. The same crooked smirk on his face. He was even dressed like Jimmy, with cuffed blue jeans and a white T-shirt under a red nylon jacket. Smitty noticed fresh abrasions on JJ's forehead, a bruised cheek, and a bandaged cut on his nose—all obviously caused by the accident the night before.

"We've never officially met, so I guess an introduction is in order," JJ began. "I'm—"

"JJ Sutton," Smitty spoke in an even tone. "I know who you are."

"You do?" JJ acted as if he was flattered, but Smitty could sense the young man's deep, dark anger. "Well, you have no idea how long I've planned and looked forward to this very moment, Sheriff."

"JJ, I want you to notice that I'm not wearing my gun." Smitty pointed to his empty holster. "I want no trouble. But I do need to take you back to town so we can sort this all out."

"Why can't we do that here?"

"I think you know why," Smitty said. "Your mom met with me this morning and told me everything."

"Did she now? Really? *Everything?*" JJ's voice had been fairly calm up until this moment. Now it was rising in tone and volume as a wave of intensity washed over his face. "She told you how hard it was being a single mom? How we had to live from paycheck to paycheck? How I heard her crying late at night? Or what it was like for me to never know my father?"

Smitty made no reply. He simply listened.

By now JJ was practically shouting. "Did she explain how hard it was to grow up knowing that the man who killed my father was still walking around free?"

"Now, wait a minute—" Smitty began.

"No! *You* wait a minute!" JJ yelled. "You can't run from this any longer. In case you haven't realized it yet, it's time to pay the piper!"

"You mean it's time for your *revenge*?"

JJ smiled down at him. "Whatever you want to call it. Both work for me."

Chapter 21

Pop, Mike, and Spence quietly walked the streets of Jubilee, listening for any signs of life from within the old buildings.

"Smitty!" Pop called out. "Where are you?"

They heard nothing but the howling of the wind.

"Let's spread out a little," Pop suggested. "Spence, you take the left side of the street. Mike, you take the right. I'll stick to the middle."

The two boys fanned out onto either side of the street as Pop continued calling: "Hello! Can anybody hear me?"

Spence thought he spotted something in the dark recesses of a nearby barn. "I wonder what's in there?"

"We should check it out," Pop said. "Mike, you'd better go with him, just in case."

Mike crossed the street and entered the dark barn with Spence. It took a few moments for their eyes to adjust to the dimly lit room, at which point they noticed two large shapes near the back wall of the barn.

"Got a light, Spence?" Mike asked.

"Not this time," Spence admitted.

"Hold on," Mike said. "I think there's another door in here."

Mike pushed at the back wall of the barn until he found what he was after. A large door swung open, and sunlight streamed into the barn. The two dark shapes they had seen were a pair of black Buick Roadmasters.

"He's here all right." Mike pointed to the nearest car, which had a long white scrape down its side. "This must be the one that knocked Smitty off the road. That's his truck's paint color on the side."

"Yeah, and the other is a backup," Spence agreed. "That makes three roadsters altogether."

"This guy wasn't taking any chances," Mike said. "He's obviously been planning this for a long time."

"Hey, Mike! Spence!" Pop called from outside the barn. "Come out here for a moment!"

The two boys joined Pop in the middle of the street.

"What is it?" Mike said, looking around.

"I could've sworn I just heard some distant shouting," Pop said. "Men's voices. But I can't tell where they are coming from."

All three listened for a few more moments, but the voices had gone silent.

Pop pointed across the street. "I think they came from somewhere over there. I'm going to check it out. You guys keep moving down the road. If you hear anything—anything at all—come back and get me. Understand?"

Both boys nodded, and the group split up.

◆ ◆ ◆

Smitty looked at the bars that now blocked all the doors and windows of the Kicking Mule Saloon.

"JJ, I don't know what you're planning to do with all this, but I want you to stop and think before you get yourself into any more trouble."

"I appreciate the concern, Sheriff. I really do." JJ picked up a nearby rope and slowly started tying. "I just find it odd that you came here to arrest me when you're the one who's guilty."

Smitty looked right at JJ. He spoke slowly and intently: "I did *not* kill your father."

"Then answer a few questions. And promise me you'll tell the truth."

"You have my word."

JJ casually looped the rope through itself. "Were you jealous of my mom and dad that night at the diner?"

Smitty paused momentarily before replying, "I was."

"Did you want to get back at my dad when you challenged him to that race?"

Smitty looked down at his feet in shame. "I did."

JJ shrugged. "We've got a motive, your honor!"

"I turned myself into local law enforcement that very night," Smitty said. "Told them everything that had happened."

"You told them how you forced my dad off the road?"

"That's *not* what happened!"

"Everyone knows my dad was the best driver around. If you didn't cause the accident, then how else can you explain what happened?"

"There was a burro in the road! Your father tried to avoid it, and he didn't make the turn!"

JJ raised his eyebrows and looked at Smitty skeptically. "A *burro*?"

"Yes!"

"And you expect me to believe that?"

"It's the truth."

JJ shook his head and chuckled. "Sorry, Sheriff. I'm just not buying it."

"I did everything I could to save your dad that night." Smitty's focus looked far away as he replayed the events in his head. "I ran down to the wreckage, but the flames . . . It was just too hot. I tried; I really did! But he . . . he was already gone."

JJ began a slow clap. "Nicely done, Smitty. Nicely done! I believe you may have missed your calling as an actor. And if I was a small-town sheriff back then, I might have believed it too."

"Listen, JJ, I'm more than willing to have the events of that night reexamined by a third party to see if I deserved a harsher judgment."

"It's too late for that, Smitty. In fact, it's over thirty years too late." JJ held up the knot he'd been tying for Smitty to see. A hangman's noose slowly swung back and forth. "It's judgment day!"

Chapter 22

Mike and Spence continued making their way down the main street of Jubilee, scanning for any sign or sound that might point them to Sheriff Smitty or JJ Sutton.

"Do you hear anything?" Spence whispered.

"No. I think maybe—" Mike froze in place and signaled for Spence to stop moving.

Both boys heard the muffled sound of distant voices. They were coming from a saloon at the end of the street.

"Go get Pop!" Mike said.

As Spence ran back the way they had come, Mike headed toward the saloon, taking care to remain out of sight. The closer he got to the saloon, the louder the voices became. Someone was shouting and obviously very angry.

While he waited for Spence to return with Pop, Mike hid in the alley next to the saloon. The sound of the raised voices was even clearer now. He looked around for an entrance, but all of the windows and doors were covered with bars. Mike guessed that the saloon was built by one of the movie companies. It was little more than a square box with no windows around the back.

The only way in Mike could find was a ladder outside—a ladder that led to a second-story loft. The door to the loft was open, with an open metal padlock hanging loosely in the door's clasp. Someone must have entered the building through this hard-to-spot entrance.

Mike climbed the ladder and carefully peered inside the saloon. From his new vantage point he could see down a corridor to what he guessed was a second-story landing. He could also see the source of the shouting: JJ Sutton held a noose and was calling down to someone on the first floor. Mike couldn't quite make out all the words, but he heard enough to know that Smitty was in trouble.

Mike pulled the loft door closed and slid the open padlock into the clasp. He kept the padlock unlocked for now; he just wanted to make sure that no one could open the door from the inside.

"He's not going to get away from us this time," Mike whispered to himself.

◆ ◆ ◆

JJ looked down on Smitty.

"After examining all the evidence and hearing your defense,

I can only come to one conclusion." JJ stared at Smitty with hate in his eyes. "Guilty."

If Smitty was afraid, he didn't show it. "Don't do this, JJ. It's not right."

"Are you ready to hear your sentence?"

"What are you planning to do?" Smitty asked. "Hang me?"

"No, that would be far too good for you." JJ dropped the noose and picked up a lit hurricane lamp. "I want you to experience the same fate as my father."

Smitty could tell that the lamp was almost completely filled with what he assumed was kerosene.

"Think about what you're doing." Smitty tried to reason with him. "You've let your hate drive you mad."

"Yes, I have," JJ said without emotion. "Good-bye, Smitty."

Without another thought, JJ threw the hurricane lamp down to the floor below. Its glass globe shattered, and the burning kerosene ignited everything it touched.

Smitty instinctively backed away from the fire. The roaring wall of flames now dashed any hopes of reaching the second-story landing.

◆ ◆ ◆

As Spence and Pop made their way toward the Kicking Mule Saloon, Mike waved at them from the alley.

"What's going on?" Pop whispered.

"JJ and Smitty are in there all right," Mike whispered back. "But we've got trouble!"

"What do you mean?" Pop asked.

"There's been a whole lot of shouting going on," Mike

explained. "And the front entrance and all the windows are covered with metal bars. I think he's got Smitty trapped in there!"

"What?" Pop wasn't sure he had heard right.

"It gets worse," Spence said. He pointed up.

Thick black smoke had started pouring out of the building.

"Oh, no!" Pop exclaimed.

◆ ◆ ◆

Avoiding the flames in the center of the room, Smitty scanned the nearby walls for any signs of weakness—anything that might allow him to escape.

"You're wasting your time, Smitty!" JJ was still gloating from the upper landing. "I reinforced those walls myself."

Most of the saloon tables were burning now, and the fire crept toward the curtains. Smitty started to cough as smoke filled the room.

"Don't worry, Smitty!" JJ yelled over the roar of the flames. "You won't have to suffer long! I've filled those barrels behind the bar with very powerful explosives!"

Smitty spotted three wooden barrels stacked together in the far corner of the room. The flames were moving toward them.

"Won't be long now!" JJ made his way back to the corridor. "Which means I must be going."

As JJ disappeared, Smitty picked up a wooden chair and swung it against the wall with all his strength. The chair splintered into pieces, yet the wall stood firm.

"Smitty!" a nearby voice yelled.

Smitty looked over to see Pop, Mike, and Spence standing just outside the barred café doors.

"Don't worry!" Mike shouted. "We're going to get you out of there."

Smitty grasped the steel bars and looked out at them. "We don't have much time. He's got some sort of high explosives in here!"

Pop turned to the boys, and Smitty heard him yell, "Mike! Spence! Look for something like a crowbar—anything we can use to help us pry open the doors. Even a two-by-four will do!"

Through the bars, Smitty could see Pop look around frantically.

"We've got to find *something*!" Pop shouted.

◆ ◆ ◆

Even as JJ Sutton made his way down the upper corridor of the saloon, he wondered why he didn't feel a greater sense of satisfaction. He had planned this exact revenge for years, yet he felt strangely empty inside.

Looking ahead, JJ noticed that the loft door was shut. Perhaps a strong gust of wind had blown it closed. He wasn't too concerned—until he discovered that the door wouldn't open. He put his full weight against it and pushed even harder. It still wouldn't open.

Now he was concerned.

"No!" he yelled as he pounded his fists against the heavy door.

JJ could hear the metal padlock rattling in the iron clasp. He realized in horror that he was locked in.

◆ ◆ ◆

Outside the saloon, Spence ran up to Pop with a three-foot steel rod.

"I found it around the corner!" Spence exclaimed. "It must've been left there by whoever barred the windows."

"This is perfect!" Pop grabbed the rod and started prying. "We'll get you out of there, Smitty!"

"You better hurry!" Smitty yelled. "That fire is getting closer to the explosives!"

"Mike! Spence!" Pop shouted. "Give me a hand! Perhaps the three of us together—!"

The boys each grabbed ahold of the steel rod.

"Give it everything you've got," Pop instructed. "Now!"

All three leaned into it and pulled at the same time.

The bars and door frame held tight.

"Again!" Pop shouted.

The boys grimaced as they pulled. Pop's face turned red. Despite their best efforts, the bars didn't even bend.

Smitty helplessly looked out at them. "It's not working, is it?"

"It's got to!" Pop repositioned the rod and began pushing from another angle. "C'mon, boys!"

They strained, pulled, and pushed, but the bars held fast. They could feel the heat building as the fire inside intensified.

Just as the situation felt hopeless, Mike dropped his hold on the metal rod, turned, and sprinted down the street.

"Mike!" Pop yelled after him. "Where are you going?"

Chapter 23

JJ Sutton made his way back down the smoke-filled corridor and reentered the saloon's second-story landing. Any hopes of reaching the other side of the saloon were dashed when he saw that the way was blocked by a wall of flames. He glanced down and saw Smitty pressed against the bars at the front entrance. He also noticed that the fire was perilously close to the explosive barrels.

Looking around frantically, JJ noticed several wooden beams that connected the landing he was standing on to the ceiling. Perhaps he could use one of them as a battering ram to smash through the loft door!

JJ immediately kicked at one of the beams. It moved a few inches.

Backing up, he lowered his shoulder and ran at it. His right shoulder exploded in pain, but the collision accomplished its purpose. JJ collapsed as the beam started to give way. Now all he had to do was . . .

The rafters above let out a horrible groan, immediately followed by a loud, splintering crack. JJ tried to get up but was slammed back down by the falling wooden beam. The pain was immense, and his situation had gone from bad to worse. He was trapped—pinned to the floor beneath the beam.

◆ ◆ ◆

Smoke billowed out the saloon's front entrance. Pop and Spence continued to try to pull against the bars, but their efforts were in vain. Smitty leaned as far forward as the metal bars would allow, gasping for fresh air. They knew the heat at his back must be unbearable.

"It's useless!" Smitty coughed. "Get away from here before this whole place blows!"

"Do as he says, Spence!" Pop shouted, even as he continued to tug.

"You too, Pop!" Smitty reached between the bars and pushed Pop away. "Get back!"

"I'm not leaving you!" Pop insisted.

Spence backed up into the street, watching helplessly. That's when he heard the rumble of an approaching car engine. He turned to see one of the phantom Buicks racing toward the saloon.

"Get out of the way!" Mike yelled from the open driver's window.

Pop ran for cover as the Buick accelerated forward on a diagonal path toward the saloon. The car struck the wooden boardwalk first, launching it slightly upward. With a loud splintering sound, the car tore through the corner of the building before coming to a stop in the side alley.

A wave of smoke poured out of the gaping hole Mike had made. Pop ran forward and caught Smitty as he came stumbling out of the saloon.

"Let's get out of here!" Smitty gasped.

Spence helped Pop lead Smitty a safe distance away.

"I thought I was a goner," Smitty admitted between coughs.

"If it wasn't for Mike . . ." Pop stopped mid-sentence and looked back toward the burning saloon. "Where *is* Mike?"

Chapter 24

Mike removed the padlock from the metal clasp and swung open the loft door. He was immediately struck by a black cloud of smoke.

He was running out of time, and he knew it. Mike quickly made his way down the upper corridor. The smoke was thick, and he couldn't see more than a couple of feet in front of him.

Mike knew Pop wouldn't approve of what he was doing. It was a huge risk, for sure. But considering all that had happened, Mike still had unfinished business to handle.

He felt the wall of heat the moment he stepped onto the second-story landing. The fire in the saloon was now a raging inferno. Hot ash floated in the air and burned his exposed skin.

"JJ!" he called. Mike stepped forward and stumbled over

something hidden by the smoke. Looking down, Mike could see that he had tripped over a heavy beam. Beneath the beam was JJ Sutton.

"Help me!" JJ pleaded. "It's got me pinned!"

Mike grabbed hold of the beam and tried to lift it off.

JJ looked up at Mike as if he was an angel sent from heaven. "Who are you?"

Mike tried to get a better grip on the beam. "I'm the one you tried to push off the cliff in Smitty's truck."

JJ's face fell. "I'm sorry. I . . . I thought you were Smitty!"

"Yeah? Well, Smitty happens to be a good friend of mine." Mike looked around hurriedly and grabbed a nearby rope. "As was Ben Jones."

JJ watched as Mike lifted the noose he had dropped earlier. "Ben Jones? Who's he?"

"He was my best friend." Mike threw one end of the rope over an overhead rafter. "The kid you ran into on the road."

"That was an accident! There was no way to stop in time!" JJ insisted. "Your friend's gonna be okay, isn't he?"

Mike loosened the noose. "Ben didn't make it."

"I never meant . . ." JJ watched with wide eyes as Mike reached forward with the open noose. "What are you *doing*? *Please! No!*"

Mike slipped the noose over one end of the beam and cinched the knot tight. Using his body as a counterweight, he grabbed the other end of the rope and pulled. The beam on top of JJ slowly started to rise.

JJ rolled away and tried to stand. "Thank you! Thank you!"

Mike helped JJ to his feet. "We gotta get out of here!"

The two stumbled down the corridor. The heat was less

intense, but the smoke seemed even thicker. Mike could hardly see or breathe, but the loft door had to be close. If they could only make it out before the explosives—

BAROOOM!

Mike felt the blast before he heard it. Both of them were pushed forward by a tornado-force wind of heat and debris. As the deafening explosion roared, the floor collapsed beneath them just as Mike and JJ tumbled out of the open loft door and down to the street below.

Mike rolled over, gasping for breath.

"Mike!" Pop ran to his grandson's side. "Are you okay?"

Mike tried to answer but could only cough. Every part of his body hurt, but he was still intact.

Smitty rolled JJ over and pulled out his handcuffs. "This one's in one piece as well."

"Oh, Mike!" Pop exclaimed. "I was so worried when we realized you had gone in after JJ!" Pop paused and looked at him soberly. "And—I've gotta admit—I was a little worried what you might do when you found him."

"I had to save him, Pop," Mike said.

Pop looked at him proudly. "I never should have doubted you."

Chapter 25

Mike was dressed in his Sunday best. His hair was combed carefully, and the somber expression on his face made him look older than his thirteen years. Spence, dressed in a suit and tie, stood to his left. Winnie, wearing a dark veil over her face, stood to his right. Smitty and Pop were behind them. Smitty removed his cowboy hat.

Once everyone was in place, Pop turned to Mike. "Go ahead."

Mike cleared his throat and began. "We are gathered here today to remember our dear friend Ben Jones."

Winnie lifted her veil and wiped her cheek.

"Ben was the kind of guy who . . . once you got to know him, you realized that despite what everyone else said about him . . ."

Mike struggled to find the right words. "He was really . . . was really a, well, um, a . . ."

Recognizing that Mike was at a loss for words, Spence put a hand on his shoulder and tried to finish the sentence for him. ". . . a dork?"

Mike looked over at Spence with a slightly surprised look on his face. "Thanks, Spence, but that's not quite the word I was looking for."

Winnie looked at Mike and solemnly suggested: "A lame-o-goob?"

Someone in the room snorted as they tried to stifle a laugh.

"That's closer, Winnie," Mike said. "But, no, I think I was going for something more along the lines of, um, a chuckle-headed dweeb!"

"Stop! Please! No more!" Ben cried out from his hospital bed. He clutched his side while wiping away tears of both laughter and pain. "It still hurts just to giggle!"

"Sorry," Winnie apologized. "But since you supposedly 'died,' it seemed only right that we give you a funeral."

Spence studied Ben closely. "Maybe he *did* die and this is only a clone!"

"Enough!" Ben laughed. "You don't understand what you're putting me through!"

"Oh yeah?" Mike reached over and affectionately ruffled his friend's hair. "Well, what do you think we went through when Arlene told us that you 'didn't make it'?"

"Goodness!" Nurse Burns shook her head in disgust as she tucked in the covers on Ben's bed. "No one from this hospital ever said anything remotely like that."

"It wasn't your fault," Pop assured her. "It was a classic

example of 'telephone.' In this case, Mrs. Bickle told Joan Farris that she had talked to Ben's mom, and that she said Ben was 'still in surgery.' Joan Farris then told Arlene that Ben 'hadn't made it out of surgery.' Of course, Arlene assumed the worse and spread it all over town that Ben just 'didn't make it.'"

"You know how Arlene is," Smitty said. "Why worry about the facts when you've got a juicy story to spread around? I hope she's learned her lesson."

Winnie sat down on the edge of Ben's bed. "Well, *I* have certainly learned a few things these past several days."

"Like what?" Ben asked.

Winnie leaned in close and looked Ben square in the eyes. "That you're one of my best friends, Ben Jones. I'll never forget that you saved my life."

Before Ben could respond, Winnie quickly kissed him on the forehead.

"Hey!" shouted Ben, as surprised as the others.

"Even if you are a chowderhead!" Winnie quickly added.

"Why'd you have to go and do that?" Ben complained, vigorously wiping the spot where Winnie kissed him.

"That's nothing," Spence said, "compared to what she did when you stopped breathing."

"Whaddya talking about?" Ben asked with a worried look on his face.

"Mouth-to-mouth," Mike said matter-of-factly.

"*No way!*" Ben exclaimed.

"And I think you kinda liked it," Spence added.

"I did not!"

"Then why didn't you stop her?" Mike asked.

"I was passed out!" Ben shouted.

"That's enough!" Nurse Burns shook a stern finger at them all. "You kids better get out of here before he really does bust his stitches."

"Ha!" Ben laughed stiffly. "You guys are just joking . . . right?"

"You heard her. Visiting hours are over." Smitty put on his trademark Stetson and headed for the door. "Say your good-byes and then skedaddle on out of here. I've gotta get back to work!"

"Let's go, everybody," Pop said.

As everyone gathered their belongings, Ben anxiously searched their faces. "Wait . . . you guys were kidding about that mouth-to-mouth stuff, right? *Right?*"

◆ ◆ ◆

Smitty was still looking back at Ben when he stepped out into the hallway. He didn't notice Donna Sutton approaching from the opposite direction until he turned and collided with her.

Donna's purse fell from her hands, spilling its contents across the hospital floor.

"Oh, Donna!" Smitty quickly knelt and started picking up whatever was in reach. "I didn't see you there."

"I didn't see you either, Smitty! I'm sorry."

"No, it was my fault. I wasn't watching where I was going."

"Arlene told me that I might find you here." Donna knelt down beside him. "I'm glad we 'bumped into' each other."

Smitty nervously glanced up at her as he dumped a few items back into her purse. He was obviously still tongue-tied around her.

"I was just coming by to thank you all for what you did for JJ," Donna said.

"It was really mostly Mike," Smitty reminded her as they both stood to their feet. "He's the one you should thank."

"I know," Donna said. "He's quite a remarkable boy."

"He is," Smitty agreed.

"The forgiveness and self-sacrifice he demonstrated made quite an impact on JJ . . ." Donna stopped to correct herself, ". . . well, on *both* of us. I also wanted to tell *you* how much I appreciate the way you spoke up for JJ at his hearing."

"I suppose it's the least I could do." Smitty looked down at his feet and nervously played with the brim of his hat. "After my involvement in what happened to his dad, I, um . . ."

"Smitty," Donna interrupted. "How long are we both going to hold on to this thing?"

Smitty was caught off guard. "Well, I don't know. I . . ."

"Don't you think, after everything that's happened, that maybe it's time we put the past behind us?"

Smitty looked at Donna, not quite sure what to say. Finally he nodded.

Donna gently touched his arm. "If it's all right, I'd love to buy you a cup of coffee sometime, and maybe catch up on old times."

Smitty hesitated at first, not sure he had heard her correctly. A smile slowly spread across his face. "I'd really like that."

"Let me walk you out to your car," Donna suggested. "Have you got something out there to write my phone number on?"

"Got a ticket pad in my glove box," Smitty suggested as they both turned and headed for the exit.

"That'll do," Donna said.

"I suppose I'd have to cite you for something first," he teased.

"Oh, really?" Donna reached across and softly slugged Smitty in the shoulder.

"Ow!" Smitty acted as if his arm was about to fall off. "That's aggravated assault on a police officer."

Donna threw her head back and laughed.

◆ ◆ ◆

Mike and Pop watched Smitty and Donna walk off together, still teasing each other and laughing.

"Never thought I'd see that in a million years!" Pop said. "Almost reminds me of what they were like back in high school."

Mike looked up at Pop. "I guess miracles really do happen."

"You're learning, Mike," Pop said. "We *both* are!"

The Last Chance Detectives will return in

Quest for the King's Crown

About the Author

Robert Vernon is the creator of the Last Chance Detectives. He produced the video series, wrote the screenplays, and directed *Legend of the Desert Bigfoot*. He also wrote and directed the Last Chance Detectives radio drama, *Last Flight of the Dragon Lady*.

Robert got his start in the entertainment industry working for television legends Johnny Carson and Dick Clark. He was a founding member of Focus on the Family's film department, where he wrote, produced, and directed many of the Adventures in Odyssey video episodes.

In 2001 he wrote and directed the feature film *Road to Redemption* for Billy Graham's World Wide Pictures. As an editor, Robert has worked on hundreds of network and cable television episodes.

Robert lives with his wife, Kristen, in Santa Clarita, California. They have three sons, one grandson, and a dog named Chance.